S0-DOO-764

HELENA HELLION

"Don't move, or you're dead men!" Spur thundered.

"You shoot me, you shoot the lady first," he said and began backing toward the other door. As Spur turned to watch Libby, another man reached for the iron on his hip.

Spur's round slashed through his shoulder and he got off a shot that went wide. Spur's second round created a neat round hole in the man's forehead going in, but splattered blood and brains over the far wall as it came out the top of his head.

Also in the *Spur* Series:

SPUR #1: ROCKY MOUNTAIN VAMP
SPUR #2: CATHOUSE KITTEN
SPUR #3: INDIAN MAID
SPUR #4: SAN FRANCISCO STRUMPET
SPUR #5: WYOMING WENCH
SPUR #6: TEXAS TART
SPUR #7: MONTANA MINX
SPUR #8: SANTA FE FLOOZY
SPUR #9: SALT LAKE LADY
SPUR #10: NEVADA HUSSY
SPUR #11: NEBRASKA NYMPH
SPUR #12: GOLD TRAIN TRAMP
SPUR #13: RED ROCK REDHEAD
SPUR #14: SAVAGE SISTERS
SPUR #15: HANG SPUR McCOY!
SPUR #16: RAWHIDER'S WOMAN
SPUR #18: MISSOURI MADAM
SPUR #19: HELENA HELLION
SPUR #20: COLORADO CUTIE
SPUR #21: TEXAS TEASE
SPUR #22: DAKOTA DOXY
SPUR #23: SAN DIEGO SIRENS
SPUR #24: DODGE CITY DOLL
SPUR #25: LARAMIE LOVERS

SPUR #19

HELENA HELLION

DIRK FLETCHER

LEISURE BOOKS NEW YORK CITY

A LEISURE BOOK®

December 2004

Published by

Dorchester Publishing Co., Inc.
200 Madison Avenue
New York, NY 10016

If you purchased this book without a cover you should be aware that this book is stolen property. It was reported as "unsold and destroyed" to the publisher and neither the author nor the publisher has received any payment for this "stripped book."

Copyright © 1986 by Chet Cunningham

All rights reserved. No part of this book may be reproduced or transmitted in any form or by any electronic or mechanical means, including photocopying, recording or by any information storage and retrieval system, without the written permission of the publisher, except where permitted by law.

ISBN 0-8439-2430-6

The name "Leisure Books" and the stylized "L" with design are trademarks of Dorchester Publishing Co., Inc.

Printed in the United States of America.

Visit us on the web at www.dorchesterpub.com.

1

The man on the road looked barely able to ride. The horse was in little better shape. Both were haggard, underfed, bone weary. The man's hair was shaggy, matted, his beard unkempt and the body odor of a dozen weeks without a bath was now overpowering. His eyes were a shade of light brown and red lines mapped most of the whites.

He lifted his head and stared down a quarter of a mile lane at the small ranch spread ahead of him. It was typical for Western Kansas. A small frame house, a larger barn and two corrals made of poles and inch-thick planks. A sixty foot Kenwood steel tower held a windmill spinning lazily in the afternoon breeze. The wind always blows in Kansas, the wanderer remembered.

He kicked the roan into motion and she walked reluctantly down the lane, then smelled water, perked up her ears, and moved faster toward the small frame house with smoke coming from the chimney.

Someone was home.

There was no blanket roll tied on the rider's saddle, no sack of provisions or clothing. The man wore a castoff homespun shirt that had all but two buttons missing. His hat had been found left in the street after a drunken brawl, and his pants had been stolen from a clothes line in Nebraska. He had put them on wet and let them dry as he wore them.

He slowed the horse. Maybe this wasn't the place.

The rider stopped the thin roan and looked around again.

Same house, same barn he had built with his two hands and strong back. New windmill, not even seven years ago could he afford a fancy four-post, angle steel tower like that. But it was over the same well he had dug a bucket full of dirt at a time. Thirty feet he had to go down.

The thin wanderer stared at the place again, then nudged the tired horse forward.

Home.

Damn! Home after such a long time.

The roan caught the scent of water in the horse trough. Yes, it was in the same place, but now it had a pipe to send the water from the pump on the windmill directly to the hundred gallon galvanized watering tank. He remembered paying almost four dollars for it back in . . . when? Must have been 1863 just before he went off to war.

He blinked to clear the moisture from his eyes.

Home!

He rode to the side door of the house and started to slide off the horse.

"Far enough mister, stay astride!" The voice came from the door and through a sliver of an opening a rifle barrel extended.

"Easy, just want to talk," the rider said.

"Talk. Who the hell are you?"

"Name is Will Walton, and this is . . . this is my ranch!"

There was a moment's silence, then the rifle lifted and the door opened. A rawboned, rail-thin man stepped out, the rifle's muzzle still centered on Will's chest.

"You a mite mixed up, stranger. This is the Bar S ranch. Sure you got the right place?"

"Damn sure. I built this house, that barn, bought the damn horse trough. Lived here until sixty-three . . ."

The man at the door lowered the rifle.

"Possible. I bought the place in sixty-six, nigh onto four years ago now. My name is Hirum Smith."

Will nodded. "Pleased to meet you . . . but this is still my ranch. Homesteaded back in . . . must have been February, sixty-three."

"Fraid not, Walton. I bought it fair and legal off this widow lady. Said she wanted to move on West. She had a hired hand named Hans, a big German guy. He went with her."

"Widow . . . don't understand. She warn't no widow."

"Said she was. Anyways I got the sale all legal, bill of sale, grant deed, whole thing recorded down at the county court house." Smith looked at him closer. "You feeling all right, mister? Look a mite peaked."

Will Walton sagged even more on his saddle. His hands shook for a minute. "You say she claimed she was a widow?"

"Yep."

"That was . . . you say four years ago . . . don't understand. Just don't . . ." Will looked up quickly. "Lying, got to be lying! You holding my woman prisoner inside? That it?"

"Easy, take it easy. I'm a bachelor. Aim to get married first of next year. Nobody's inside. Bought this place fair and square."

Will shook his head, then shivered. It couldn't have been four years! The war is just over, not a month ago. Got mustered out and headed home. Yes, he got held up a time or two. It was all so mixed up.

He scowled, looked back at Smith. "What year did you say it was when you bought my ranch?"

"Back in sixty-six."

"And that was how long ago?" Will asked.

"Christ! Don't you even know what year it is? This is eighteen and seventy. Whole new decade and U.S. Grant is our president. A Republican, by God!"

Will shook his head. "Can't be five years since the war was over. Ain't taken me five years to ride home. What's going on? Am I crazy or something?"

"Easy there. You were a soldier. War did funny things to some men. I was there, too. Got wounded and discharged early on. Say, you want to lite a spell and have something to eat? Look like you could use it. Come in and I'll tell you all I know about the folks who lived here. Woman said she was a war widow, lost her husband at the Wilderness she said. She had a boy, said his father never saw the lad. He was two or three at the time, I guess."

"A boy? She had a boy? This woman who was short and fat and had long yellow hair?" It hit him as nothing had since the war. A new wave of joy and wonder swept over him. He had sired a son!

Will sat there shaking his head. "Five years. You say I been wandering around for five years? Ain't possible. Just can't be!" He slid from his horse, staggered and Smith caught him by one shoulder.

"Yeah, come in and I'll heat up some of the stew I

made. Damn good stew. Sure looking forward to a woman's cooking again, but this ain't half bad. Sit and rest and I'll tell you everything I remember about the woman and her son.

"This Martha was a short woman, little on the plump side, with long wheat straw color hair."

Two hours later former Lt. William Walton of the Ohio 25th Infantry Regiment, thanked the rancher for the meal and information. They had watered his horse and given her a muzzle bag filled with oats.

Then he rode into town. Plainview wasn't much of a settlement. Two hundred people called it home and even that number was going down. Seemed like everything clustered around the railroad, and the new magic tracks were far to the south of Plainview.

Will stood on the boardwalk in front of the general store. He saw two men he knew, but they walked by without a second glance at him. The third man looked again and held out his hand.

"Will! Damn good to see you. Haven't seen you for years. Damn good to talk again. You are looking a mite sickly, Will. Better take care of your health. Sorry I have an appointment at the bank about a loan." The man in the black suit and fancy vest hurried down the street.

"I'm glad to be back," Will said after him, but the man kept walking. In the Cattleman's Saloon he found a familiar face behind the bar.

"Jesus, Mary and Joseph, look who done come back from the dead! Will Walton!" Charley held out a meaty hand. "Damn, they all said you was dead. Wilderness got you I heard. Pretty little wife of yours sold the ranch and moved some damn place."

"I'm finding out," Will said. "Look, I ain't got a penny on me . . ."

"Beer's on the damn bar," Charley said. He was a

grossly fat man, short, naturally stout and when fueled with beer he ballooned. He drew the brew and pushed it before Will.

The ex-army officer had to blink back tears so they wouldn't show. A real man didn't cry, leastwise not in public. He sipped the beer.

"Christ, Will. Guess you're trying to find your woman. Didn't hear where she was heading. West though, as I remember. She took along that foreman she had. Hans somebody. Damn big German who could drink twenty beers and walk a straight line. Never seen a beer drinker like him. Never got filled up. Every twenty minutes by the clock he used the privy out back. That son of a bitch could drink beer all night!"

"Out West? Martha moved out West. Damn big place, Charley."

"Best I can do. Heard they was heading west."

Will spent a half hour with the beer, nursing it, reveling in a luxury he hadn't had in months. It was all he could do to get odd jobs to find enough to eat. He rode the grub line whenever he could, moving from ranch to ranch asking for work.

It was the Code of the West. A hungry man was never turned away from a ranch cook house. Ranch owners and hands knew that someday they could be in the same fix, and so they fed the grub line riders and wished them well.

An hour before dark, Will thanked Charley for his kindness and rode out of town. He stopped in a clump of trees next to a small stream and made a fire to stay warm as night descended. He was just ready to curl up with his head against his saddle as a pillow, when he thought about the war. Had it really been five years since the war was over? Where had the time gone? What had he been doing all those years? Why couldn't he remember? His hand rubbed the scar on the back of his head.

He knew he joined the army in sixty-three. Then he fought and bled and recuperated and fought again. He got out in sixty-five, he was sure of that. The smoke drifted into his eyes, and for a moment he thought of the Wilderness.

Lt. Will Walton lifted his pistol when he heard cannon fire and he went flat on the ground, his eyes staring into the brush, the thickets. There were Rebels out there! He knew there were. What did the generals know?

His commander, Colonel Richardson, said he had scouting reports of masses of troops less than a half mile from the XI Corps' front lines. Not even Brigadier General Nathanial McLean thought there could be any kind of a flanking attack without some of his own scouts reporting Rebel movement.

Lt. Will Walton lay beside his men on the picket line. They could see no more than ten yards ahead in most places because of the thick brush, thorn bushes, vines and saplings.

Will knew the Confederate skirmishers were getting closer. He could *hear the bastards moving!* His men reported shots, quite a few, but the woods so hushed the sounds that it was almost impossible to tell from what direction the sound came. Will was positive that none of the generals or their colonels could hear the shots or they would be moving troops to meet the advance.

Lt. Walton talked quietly to his men.

"Hold steady. The colonel himself told me that no sane man would try a mass attack through that wilderness of brush out there. Those thorn bushes would cut up a division."

A twenty round barrage of fire sounded almost directly in front of them and Lt. Walton saw one of his men go down.

"Keep low and hold your fire!" Lt. Walton bellowed.

"The colonel told us nobody is out there," a Yankee private whispered.

"Hell, the same colonel told us nobody could attack through the brush and brambles either," a sergeant snarled. "But the damn Rebels are coming!"

A wild falsetto Rebel yell shattered the silence, then a sound the men hated crashed in on them, the ominous roll of hundreds of weapons firing as the infantry charged forward.

Lt. Walton scanned the brush. No figures yet. Ten yards! Rifle bullets sang through the air around them. He dug lower into the mulch of the woodsy floor.

"Fire when you see them!" Lt. Walton cried at his men of the Third Company.

Six rifles went off at once. The nervous soldiers hastily reloaded.

Six Rebel grey uniforms jolted through the brush directly ahead of them. Rifles cracked and roared. The six men were replaced by twenty more then those by twenty more and soon a solid wall of Rebels stormed over the brush and the bodies of their own men, trampling everything into the ground, sweeping over the hastily set up Yankee picket line.

"Back!" Lt. Walton shouted. Only four men from his forty staggered to the rear, firing at the surging gray uniforms behind them. A round caught Lt. Walton in the thigh. He plunged on. He saw two of his men explode as an artillery shell hit to his left. Only a spray of red mist was left of the men as he stormed ahead.

Everywhere he saw running Yanks, some trying to fire behind them, some trapped when they had built fortifications facing the wrong way. The enemy had swept both flanks and got behind the main force.

He heard that Von Gilsa's skirmish line of two German regiments was swept away by a screaming, bellowing mass of Rebels who charged forward like wild men, smothering all resistance in front of them.

Word spread among the survivors that Colonel Lee and Colonel Reily's regiments were soon battered and routed. Within minutes General Charles Devens' whole division had collapsed and men were streaming to the rear, making no pretense of fighting.

Will swung around and stared down the long road. It was a floor of blue uniforms. Behind him he saw that the two "knuckle" guns which had been positioned to protect his flank, had been swung around by Rebels and they were firing them down the road with grape and canister and anything they could ram down the barrel. It was a slaughter.

He heard the cannon go off and dove into the ditch just as a six-inch length of railroad tie slammed into a corporal's chest three feet to his left, tearing the torso in half, and dumping him against a tree where he hung as if nailed there.

Will plowed into the brush twenty feet, then ran north following the edge of the roadway, away from the death, away from the blood. His leg burned like fire where the rifle ball had penetrated. He limped and then staggered. He found a branch to use as a crutch.

Behind him the Rebel tide rolled forward. On the road he had heard a captain say that Stonewall

Jackson had hit the soft spot in the Yankee lines with twenty-eight thousand men, and nothing could stop them.

At last Will fell behind a tree. He could run no farther. Struggling over pain and horror he had moved back far enough so he was out of the heavy fighting. Either that or the Rebs had all surged around him. He was near the Chancellorville house somewhere but off the road still hidden in the brush. He wrapped up his bleeding leg the best he could. There was no chance to get medical attention. Whole regiments had been wiped out, companies ground under the surge of the Rebels. Everything was massive confusion since the back areas had become the fighting zones.

Most commands were disorganized, frantic and confused. Rebel troops had overrun and bypassed thousands of Yankees. He still had a pistol on his hip. He drew it now and huddled against the felled tree.

A dozen men passed by five yards from him but in the half light of dusk they could not see him. He didn't know if they were friends or foe. He waited another hour, tried to determine which way to the river, but could not.

Someone staggered toward him, turned and fell almost at his feet. It was totally dark now, the brush cutting out most of the faint moonlight.

Will stared at the man for several minutes. He did not move. Slowly Will crawled up to him. In a splash of light through the heavy brush he made out the gray tunic. The man was a Rebel!

Will pulled his four-inch knife he had brought from Kansas and lifted it to strike, when the Rebel mumbled something.

Will pulled back his hand. The Rebel's eyes

flickered open.

"Water!" the man whispered.

Will found his canteen still on his belt. He tipped it and gave the enemy a drink. Now he could make out his face better. He was maybe twenty-one or two. His uniform was torn, a bloody slash across one arm and his chest was a mass of blood.

Will stared at him. The eyes watched him with fear.

"Yank?"

"Yes."

"Looks like we're both shot up."

"Yes. How can you even talk?"

"Most can't. I'm . . ."

He coughed, spitting up blood.

Will raised his hand. "Don't talk, and I don't want to know who you are, or where you're from."

The Rebel watched him. He had no weapons showing. The man's eyes mirrored pain and he closed them a moment. Then they jolted open, the fear plain.

"You'll aiming to kill me?"

"Seems to be the general idea. Your boys killed all of my company."

"That's what they tell us to do."

A moment later the air buzzed with rifle rounds as two forces began firing at each other. Both men pressed into the ground. Will pulled his pistol, but he saw no soldiers from either side.

The shooting and shouting soon died out.

"Get on with it you gonna kill me. I ain't got . . . but a few hours anyway. Coughing blood . . . always good as dead. Seen two buddies die that way. Use . . . the knife, quieter."

"I'm not going to kill you, soldier."

'Your job. You being an . . . officer and all."

"Forget it. You know where your lines are?"

"Ain't no lines. Advanced so fast, lost contact with both sides. Don't know where . . . the hell we are." He wheezed and spit up blood again. But went on. "Then I got hit bad, some canister . . ."

"Reb, I've got to move. Back north to the river. Your people will find you in the morning."

"Not a chance. Be stiff dead then." Tears seeped down his cheeks. "Don't matter. Hurt most gone . . . that's bad sign. Watched too many wounded die. Hell, don't matter. I never 'mounted to much nohow. You best get. Us Rebs own this hill . . . and woods. Stay off the road. Damn death trap." He coughed again.

"Oh, Jesus!" the man whispered, then spewed blood from his mouth in a thick red torrent. He looked at Will once more, then sighed and his eyes closed in pain, then drifted open but he saw only eternity.

Will slid away from him, and stood. He used the cane and hobbled north, he hoped it was north. Then the bullets began to fly again and he dropped to the ground. It was cold.

The cold of the ground penetrated his hands and chest. Will shook his head. Where was he? Not at the Wilderness, damn sure. He held a saddle, smelled a fire. Damn, he'd done it again! The war was over. He was in Kansas in his camp, just outside of Plainview, and somebody *was shooting* at him.

"Don't reach for that six-gun or you're deader than a headless rattler!" a man growled.

Will looked up slowly. The man in the faint firelight was grubby, hair matted, teeth black and gone, beard as scruffy and ragged as Will's. But he held the gun.

Another man strode in, kicked away Will's Colt and picked it up.

"Nice piece," he said softly and pushed it in his belt. Then he reached down and backhanded Will in the face.

"Stand up and take off your clothes 'till you're mother naked."

Will hesitated. The man kicked him in the side. Will tumbled to the ground from his half kneeling position, then stood quickly.

"Strip, asshole!" the first man said and fired into the ground between Will's boots. Will pulled off his tattered homespun shirt, then wiggled out of the pants and tossed them to one side.

"Time enough?" the younger one asked.

"Hell no, he's too old. Wait for a young one."

The older robber watched Will carefully. "Now your boots and socks. Rush it!" Will pulled off his boots standing up. They were too big and fit him loosely. He shivered in the chill.

"Flat on your belly, arms over your head," the younger one ordered Will. He stretched out. For a moment he could see neither man, then they laughed. One whistled and horses trotted up.

A moment later they had mounted and both guffawed again, then wheeled and rode off, shooting twice into the air.

Will sat up cautiously. They were gone. So were all of his clothes, his meager sack of food, his saddle and his horse. He was alone and naked and didn't own a penny's worth of anything, not even a homespun shirt! But for once he was absolutely sure where he was and what he was going to do.

He had to find his family! Naked or not, he had to find where Martha had gone and where she had taken his son. Because now for the first time he knew he had a son. An heir! Every man wants a son. He had a reason to get a new ranch and build it up, he had a son!

The headache came and without thought he touched the scar deep in his hair where the rifle bullet had slashed through the back of his head. It had been deep enough to cause him severe problems and pain, but not deep enough to kill him. How often he wished that the lead had killed him in the Wilderness.

Will Walton sat on the cold ground and looked at the few yellow lights in Plainview. He had to find his family, he had to find his son! Now he had a great reason. He rubbed his head without thinking and the unseen harpies flew around him bringing a headache that almost made him scream.

Instead he smiled. He had to find his son!

2

Spur McCoy sat in the stagecoach and bounced along over the rutted trail as the Concord coach did its best to absorb as much of the shock as possible. The Concord was the best stage coach made, the standby of the Wells Fargo Overland Stage routes.

Now Spur was luxuriating in the space. On three upholstered benches inside the coach as many as nine passengers were often seated. The center bench was always the hardest to ride, and the last occupied, since there was no back rest to lean on.

But now there were only three passengers on the stage, all headed to Helena, Territory of Montana and the end of the line. There was no easy riding railroad up this high in the United States.

Two lines were starting to work to put in northern rail service, but nothing was past the talking stages yet. Spur rode the trains as often as possible now in his job as a United States Secret Service man. But he marveled at the quality of this land schooner he rode.

In these days when a cowboy made $25 a month

and found, the Concord coaches cost as much as
$1,500, and were all built in Concord, New Hamp-
shire at the Abbot-Downing factory.

Their best features were the thoroughbraces, a
pair of wide suspension straps an inch thick that
served to absorb many of the jolting shocks of the
road. This often created a rocking motion that some
people objected to, but Spur said it lulled him to
sleep like a good rocking chair.

Depending on the territory, four to six horses
pulled the rig, commanded by the driver who sat up
front on the box. Below him was the leather enclosure known as the front boot where mail, express,
and valuables were kept during transit. Luggage
was packed on top or in the rear boot, which was
larger than the front one.

Spur shifted his weight and looked out the
window. He knew it took six horses on this part of
the run to pull the Concord up to Helena, which sat
at more than four thousand feet above sea level, and
not far from the famous Rocky Mountains. He had
never been to Helena before, and he might not come
back until they had a respectable railroad.

They had left the gamma grass and bunch grass
behind on the edge of the Great Plains, and wound
through foothills and small mountains as they
worked higher into the center of Montana.

There was game enough to satisfy any sportsman.
From the rocking coach that day Spur had seen two
kinds of deer, a bouncing antelope herd of ten, as
well as puma or mountain lion, which quickly moved
into cover. There were black bear, moose, grizzly
bear and wolves in the higher reaches of the
mountains as well.

The forests were magnificent with Douglas fir,
ponderosa pine and western larch mixed with

lodgepole pine and Engelmann spruce.

But right then Spur was more interested in getting to Helena, settling a small problem and getting back to a real law problem. He snorted as he thought of his assignment:

"PROCEED TO HELENA, MONTANA TERRITORY. MEET WITH LIBBY ADAMS WHO HAS BEEN LIFE-THREATENED. PROTECT HER, BRING TO JUSTICE ANY LAWBREAKERS IN THIS MATTER, YOUR LENGTH OF STAY THERE AT HER DISCRETION. BY ORDER OF WILLIAM WOOD, DIRECTOR OF THE SECRET SERVICE. CONFIRM."

A second wire from General Halleck, the number two man in the agency and Spur's usual boss, explained matters a little more fully.

The woman in question, a rich widow, was stirring up a fuss about women's rights, and demanding the vote. She had the right to complain, but there was no chance she would succeed. She also was a personal friend of William Wood, and Spur WOULD WITHOUT FAIL allow her to campaign for women's suffrage, protecting her at all times until they both felt the danger to her life was over.

Spur sighed and looked out at the trail ahead. They were working downward, which meant they were coming off the mountains into Prickly Pear valley, where Helena was located. He looked out the window and ahead could see smoke drifting into the sky and the outline of buildings three miles away. They should arrive in time for him to take a bath before supper. It had been a long trip from the train at Rawlings, Wyoming.

When the stage pulled into Helena it was a festive occasion. The big red and gold coaches came only twice a week and brought mail, a little freight and mail order goods from the big catalogs.

A dozen dusty boys ran alongside the coach the last block to the Wells Fargo station. The driver heaved back on the reins and the sweating horses came to a stop as the shotgun guard above clamped down on the big rear wheel brakes.

Spur let the woman get out first, then the drummer who had his showcase of fine knives and cutlery with him in the coach. He would not trust it on top.

When Spur stepped into the inch-deep dust on Helena's Main Street, he avoided the horse droppings. The shotgun guard on top tossed him down his carpetbag. Spur caught it and headed for the boardwalk that fronted the row of shops and stores.

Helena was a big town for Montana, with more than 3,500 souls—half of them still looking for gold, the other half in lumbering or cattle or farming, and the rest trying to satisfy the retail needs of everyone.

A strange sound assailed Spur's ears. He looked down the street and saw an interesting sight. Wagons and horses cleared the wide dusty avenue to make way for a parade of sorts. Six or eight women all wearing pure white blouses with long sleeves and dark skirts marched up Main Street waving banners.

In front and beside them marched a ten piece German band with tubas and trumpets.

Spur got to the boardwalk and watched the marchers. The first sign he could read said: "The Vote For Women Now!" The next one read: "We Pay Taxes, Too!" then "Taxation Without Representation!" There were two of each kind of the neatly painted signs being carried by the women.

Men hooted at them from the boardwalks.

"Get home and get my supper ready!" one man shouted. Men laughed and clapped. Women on the sidewalk stared, laughed embarrassed, or turned away. A few shouted in favor and went and joined the parade.

"You get my pants sewed up yet, Katy?" a man called. One of the marchers turned, her face red.

"No Barney, I didn't. And you'll be sleeping in the stables for the next week!"

Then everyone hooted at Barney, who wasn't sure the whole thing was so much fun anymore.

Spur looked at the woman leading the pack. Tall, midnight black hair, a proud carriage and a slender, enticing body. She had to be Libby Adams.

Spur watched the lady, the way she walked, the way she bounced her sign up and down and stared hard at the men along the boardwalk. As she passed by him their eyes locked for a moment and then she moved on.

A drunk staggered off the board walk, tripped, rolled forward and then stumbled and crashed into Libby Adams. Spur jumped of the wooden walk and darted into the street. He picked up Libby Adams, nodded, then grabbed the drunk and dragged him twenty feet to the horse trough.

Spur upended the man, held him by the ankles and dunked him head first into the wooden horse drinking tank. The man sputtered pushed up with his hands, roaring in protest. Spur dunked him in again, then dropped him lengthwise in the water to the roar of approval of the marchers and audience alike.

The march, which had stopped when Libby went down, began again, the band playing, the women

waving their banners. Libby looked at Spur and
smiled, nodded, then marched forward waving her
placard.

Spur stepped up on the boardwalk as a man came
through the crowd and stared at Spur. The big man
tensed, then saw the watcher smile. He came
forward and held out his hand.

"You got to be Spur McCoy, right?"

Spur took the hand in a sold shake. "True, just
got off the stage. I didn't get your name."

"Sheriff Josiah Palmer of Lewis and Clark
County. We should have a talk. I got a letter that
said you might be coming."

"Word travels fast. That lady in front of the line is
Libby Adams?"

"Yep, just wish she'd stay in that big house of
hers or in her bank. Getting tired of these parades."

"Legal though, right?"

"True, unless they get disruptive or violent, then
I can refuse a parade permit. Oh, yes, we have laws
here too, McCoy." He nodded to the left and both
men turned that way.

A shot slammed through the sound of the oompha
band and Spur spun looking back at the street.
Libby cried out in pain and fell backwards into the
other women who caught her. Blood smeared her
left arm.

Spur and the sheriff ran into the street. Spur
looked to the left where he thought the shot came
from. An alley opened there and before anyone else
could move, Spur charged through the crowd and
down the alley. New brick buildings showed on both
sides at Main Street. Then there was a void before
he came to houses on the next block.

He saw no one. He stopped but there were no
frantic hoof beats of an escaping bushwhacker. He

saw something ahead, a nearly new red handkerchief tied into a neck band. Nothing else. He ran back through the alley, checking trash barrels and boxes, but no one hid in any of them.

The shooter either went into one of the side doors of the stores, into the houses or through the empty area between them. No chance to catch him now.

When Spur got back to the street, the sheriff led Libby along the boardwalk to a doctor's office.

Spur followed and took off his hat when he came to the door. McCoy was a big man at six-two and an even two hundred pounds. He was tanned and fit from spending more time outdoors than under a roof. His reddish brown hair was longish, fighting with his shirt collar, hiding part of his ears. On the sides he wore half mutton chops with the sideburns below his ears.

His upper lip sported a neatly trimmed half-inch wide moustache. Right now his hands were hard and rough from doing some rope work on a cattle spread. He was an excellent horseman, journeyman cowboy, crack shot with rifle and pistol and he practiced twenty rounds a day when he could get the time.

He pushed open the medic's door and stepped inside. There was no office as such, just a plain room with benches around three walls. Through an open door he saw Libby sitting in a chair. Spur moved to the door and looked in.

"Doctor Harriman, I'm not about to die," Libby Adams said. "Just bandage it up so I can get back with my ladies and finish the march."

"Afraid not, Mrs. Adams," Sheriff Palmer said. "I cancelled the rest of the march . . . violence. Part of the conditions you must remember."

"But . . ."

Spur moved so he could see the whole room. Libby

sat on a chair and Doctor Harriman looked at the wound on her bare upper left arm.

"Ouch! Oh, that hurts, Doc."

"Going to hurt a lot more if you don't hold still," Doc Harriman growled. "Got to be sure that the slug went right through."

"With two holes in her arm, it's a good possibility," Spur said. They all turned to look at him.

Sheriff Harriman spoke up quickly like the good politician he was.

"Libby Adams, like you to meet Spur McCoy. Your dang fooled notions is why he's here. This old sawbones is Doc Harriman."

Spur nodded at the woman. "Saw your parade."

"Should I know you?" she asked, her voice smooth, pleasant somehow amused.

"McCoy is the gent sent out by Washington to keep an eye on you, just like your little friend, Governor Benjamin F. Potts said they would," Sheriff Palmer said in a neutral voice.

"Thank you Josiah, I absolutely will not fight with you today. I got shot so I should be a heroine. I'd much rather talk to this nice Mr. McCoy who rescued me not once, but twice. Are you really from Washington D.C.?" she asked.

Spur grinned. "No Ma'am. I'm from St. Louis."

"Oh?" She was disappointed.

"But I work for William Wood, who I would guess is a good friend of Governor Potts. My official title is United States Secret Service Agent, and I'm at your service."

"Well, isn't that nice?" Libby smiled. Her soft brown eyes sparkled and her smile showed even, white teeth. She was a pretty woman, striking, self assured, and, he remembered, rich. She swirled her long hair around her shoulders and turned so she could stare at Spur as the doctor worked on her arm. Apparently she had forgotten about it.

Spur knew how painful an arm wound like that could be. He saw her wince only once as the doctor completed his probing of the wound, then began to treat and bandage the violations.

"You're much younger than the expert I expected, Mr. McCoy."

Spur laughed, watching her eyes. "Thank you. And you are much prettier than what I expected."

It was her turn to laugh. "Pretty is as pretty does," she said. She looked down at her arm. "Thanks, Doc. Sorry I was such a crybaby."

He reached up and kissed her cheek. "Libby, you took that better than nine out of ten cowpokes I patch up." He looked at the sheriff and Spur. "I'm over sixty, so I get to give all my pretty patients a kiss on the cheek. Part of my day, actually." Before he could move, Libby reached over and kissed his weathered cheek, then stood.

When she lifted her left arm, a small yelp of wonder seeped from her lips.

"Yep, gonna hurt a mite before it heals. Just no heavy lifting or pitching hay or digging graves. Outside that, Libby, you should be fine."

She smiled at him and stood in front of Spur.

"Mr. McCoy, I wouldn't mind at all if you wanted to treat me to some ice cream over at the Helena General Store. They just put in a new machine that makes it, but they can't keep it frozen very long in the ice box. I heard they made some this morning, game?"

"I haven't had any ice cream since I was last in Denver," Spur said holding out his arm to her good right hand. "I just hope they made strawberry."

She caught his elbow and they walked the two blocks along the boardwalk to the general store. There were half a dozen people around a small table at the back of the store where a clerk with a white apron was dishing out ice cream.

The people parted when Libby came up. The clerk looked at her and smiled.

"Not quite as firm as it was when you were here this morning Mrs. Adams. But I like it better softer."

"Two of your large sized dishes, Lester," she said. Spur fished in his pocket for change and came up with four quarters.

"Nickel a dish," Lester said setting the soup dishes filled with creamy vanilla on the counter. Spur gave him the quarter and carried both dishes to a free spot around the table.

"Seconds on ice cream today, Mrs. Adams?"

"My one vice," she said looking at him. She smiled mischievously. Her voice lowered. "No, that's just one of my vices."

As they ate the ice cream, Spur was surprised and pleased. She was not at all what he had expected.

"You're serious about getting the vote for women?"

"Of course. Women had the vote in New Jersey from 1790 to 1807. Then the men 're-interpreted' the state constitution. I bet you didn't know that the first national convention on women's suffrage was held in 1850 in Worcester, Massachusetts."

"Afraid I was too busy to attend that one," Spur said.

"Don't patronize me, Spur McCoy. I'm deadly serious."

"That's my job, keep you serious but not dead."

She licked off her spoon and stared at him. "I'm

not sure yet how to know what you mean when you talk that way. But I'll figure it out. I'm a fast learner. I bet you didn't know that right now, today, there is one territory where women have the vote. Do you know that?''

"Which one?"

"Wyoming, of course. They got the right to vote from the beginning. The very first legislature voted on December tenth last year to extend the right of the ballot to all women over twenty-one years of age in the state!''

"A person can learn something new every few days," Spur said.

"Now I understand. You *are laughing* at me." She stood. "I don't like people who laugh at me. I hope you don't continue this when you come to supper at my house tonight. We will serve promptly at eight. Come at seven. We will have a chance to do some planning about security, and what you think you can do to protect me. I'll see myself out and home, thank you.''

Spur watched her leave, then finished his ice cream. It was delicious.

An hour later Spur had made all the needed arrangements and had a metal bathtub brought to his room along with the five pails of hot water. It was scald yourself first and freeze toward the end of the bath.

He had been on the road for a week getting to Helena. A week of sweating and grime and the second class accommodations at the few stage stopovers they had. Now he wanted a bath and some clean clothes before he crossed swords with Libby Adams again. He smiled as he stepped into his bath. That Libby Adams was one hell of a woman, and she knew it.

Spur could sit in the long, narrow tub and extend his legs, but not lie down. It was enough. He soaked, then scrubbed and soaked again. After three scrubbings he decided at least half of the grime was gone.

McCoy dressed in clean blue pants and matching dark jacket, then he pushed the tub and buckets into the hall and searched out a barber shop. He had a fresh shave and a haircut to bring his wild hair into more control and a moustache trim. Then he moved on to the best saloon in town and asked questions about Libby Adams.

The barkeep grinned.

"One hell of a woman, that one!" he said. "You see her this afternoon marching, shouting, and then when she got shot she never cried or wailed or even said it hurt! Make a damn good soldier that woman." The apron shrugged. "Course it don't hurt that she's the richest lady in town. Richer than any of the men as well. She owns the bank and about half the retail businesses.

"Hell, when the town burned down last year, she started putting up new stores before the damned ashes was cool!"

Spur took a pull on the lukewarm beer. "How did she get all of her money, property?"

"Married it. Some folks put her down for that, don't bother me. Hell, she did right by old Phil for as long as he lived." The bartender motioned Spur closer. "See, she was twenty-one or twenty-two, and old Phil was sixty-one when she married him. Didn't make no difference to either of them.

"She kept his books, and tended his house and helped him with business for five years. Then one night old Phil climbed on top of her and got too damned excited. Doc says the old boy went out with a hardon that wouldn't stop. He just plain fucked himself to death!"

"That the story?" Spur asked.

"Hell, no story, God's truth. Undertaker said the old boy was buried with a hardon. First time he'd ever seen it."

They both chuckled and Spur looked at the time. It was a quarter to seven. He asked the barkeep where her house was, gave him a fifty cent tip and walked up the street and down a block to the biggest, fanciest, most ostentatious mansion in Helena.

At eight o'clock in Helena that time of summer, it's still daylight. When Spur was still two blocks from the big house, he sensed someone behind him, and stepped quickly into an alley. A moment later two men ran down the street toward him. Both held pistols. Spur dropped back deeper into the alley and waited. The first came in fast and flattened against a brick wall behind a large trash barrel.

The second came forward as if to draw Spur's fire, then darted backward. He slid around the corner out of danger. A half a minute later the man at the mouth of the alley ran in and rolled toward the same protection where the first man had vanished.

Spur leaned out and blasted three rounds at the tumbling man. He was not sure if he hit him, but then he had another problem. Before he could move back to the protection of the large cardboard boxes, he saw an object hurled toward him. He had seen small hand bombs during the war.

This looked like a homemade variety. He guessed that two sticks of dynamite had been tied together. The fuse sputtered in the air and Spur figured it would fall near where he lay. He dove under a pair of two by twelve timbers that had been nailed together and leaned against the wooden wall of the store.

A second later the bomb went off with a cracking roar and hundreds of pieces of metal slammed into the boxes and the boards. Spur crawled out and waited, his six-gun ready. He heard cautious steps. One man looked around the cardboard box which Spur saw had been riddled as if by shrapnel. When the head peered over the protection, Spur shot him in the forehead, then jumped up.

The second man ran toward the alley. Spur leveled in and held the weapon with both hands and fired twice. Both slugs caught the man in the shoulders and slammed him to the ground.

Spur looked at the riddled boxes again, shook his head and ran forward to the downed man. He had lost his weapon. Spur rolled him over with one boot. He had never seen the man before.

"Who sent you to kill me?" Spur asked.

The man snorted.

Spur put his boot on the shot up shoulder and pressed down. A scream of pain slanted through the alley.

"Who?" Spur asked again.

"Just a man. Never knew who he was."

Spur kicked the shot shoulder, and the man screamed again.

"I can hold out much longer than you can," Spur spat. "I'd say you'll bleed to death in about fifteen minutes."

The man remained silent. Spur knelt before him and backhanded him across the mouth, then jolted the shoulder. For a moment the gunman almost passed out.

He looked at Spur with hatred. "True, never saw the man before. Said he was from out of town. Told me I could earn an easy fifty dollars. I got help.

Didn't know you was a one man army. How did you get away from that dynamite with roofing nails taped around it?"

"Easy," Spur snarled. "Now what was the man's name?"

"Might have been a fake name. Said he was from Virginia City if I was in that area. Said his name was Laidlaw."

Spur hoisted the man to his feet and marched him over to Doc Harriman's office. He told the doctor to patch him up and hold him for the sheriff. Charge: attempted murder.

"I'd wait for the sheriff, but I'm late for a dinner engagement with a beautiful black haired lady."

Doc Harriman chuckled. "Guess I can manage. Just wish I was going to dinner up there in your place."

Spur was twenty minutes late getting to dinner at Libby Adam's big mansion.

3

Spur McCoy started to lift the fancy knocker on the front door of the Adams mansion when the massive panel unlatched and swung inward. Before him stood Libby Adams.

There was only one word Spur thought of, so he said it softly, with surprise an awe.

"Dazzling!" She was. Libby had prepared, too. Her hair was swept up and piled on top of her head making her appear nearly six feet tall. The richly decorated dress she wore touched the floor but left uncovered both shoulders and plunged deeply between her breasts showing the sides of both firm mounds. The dress pinched in at the waist and curved out over good hips before falling to cover her shoes.

Her face was radiant, with only a little rouge and a touch of red on her lips. She smiled.

"Mr. McCoy, I presume?" She smiled. "Won't you come in? My, you look so much more handsome than you did this afternoon. A haircut and shave do help, don't they?"

Spur found his voice at last and stepped inside to a thick rug, and a beautifully decorated entrance-way. Doors led off in three directions.

"Are you sure this is the same woman's rights marcher I saw shot and then dumped into the dust this afternoon in Main Street?"

She laughed and caught his hand. "The same. I enjoy dressing up when there's someone to dress up for. You are extremely naughty, you know, you're quite late."

"Sorry, I was held up."

She led him down a short hallway with a carpet runner on the floor and original oil paintings on the walls. At the second door she went into a large square room that held a six foot walnut table set up for a banquet for two.

"Before we talk business, we have supper; dinner, some people in New York call it. I hope that out here in the rough frontier we can be elegant enough for you."

"This will do nicely. I haven't seen anything this elaborate since a dinner reception for the Duke of York in the White House in Washington D.C. during the war."

"She smiled. "Thank you, I'm delighted that you're impressed." They sat down and then the food began to come. It was a seven course meal with appetizers, soup, salad, then an entree of fresh fish followed by steak and four kinds of vegetables, followed by three courses of deserts.

At last Spur pushed away from the table.

"I don't think I can even stand I ate so much," he said. "I had forgotten how much I had missed good food on the stage coming up here. Do you know it took me eight days to get here from the railroad?"

"Yes, I remember. Eight days of little sleep and

less food. I came in that way myself, about a thousand years ago. Let's move into the drawing room for some business."

When they were seated in strikingly upholstered chairs looking through a window into a carefully tended garden, Libby stared at him.

"Spur McCoy, I was shot today. Does that mean someone is really trying to kill me, or only to scare me?"

Spur stood and walked to the window, then came back. "Either way, it's my job to stop them. I want you to clear with me before you make any talks in public or go on any more marches. That slug through your arm could just have easily been through your pretty little head. You take no more chances until I find out who fired that shot."

"Yes, sir."

"That easy?"

"Who wants to get shot? I never argue with experts. I make it a rule always to find the best people in the field and follow their suggestions."

"That doesn't sound very liberated. What about all of the woman suffrage work? What about Elizabeth Cady Stanton and Susan B. Anthony?"

"Who are they?"

"Suffragettes in the east. Oh, I have another name for you. On my way here two gentlemen insisted that I do one thing, but I didn't want to."

"What was it they wanted you to do?"

"Die." He told her about the brief encounter with death in the alley.

"So far one man has died in this little drama. I don't want you to be the second corpse. The man who lived agreed to my logic and told me who had hired him. I wondered if you might know him. He's from Virginia City, evidently."

"I do know some people there. What was his name?"

Spur watched her closely. "The man who was mentioned was someone with the last name of Laidlaw."

Her reaction was instant.

"Oh, damn! I never thought he would go this far." She stopped. "But the men who shot at you, may not have been the same ones who shot at me."

"True, I'll ask the gentleman about that first thing tomorrow. Now, what about Mr. Laidlaw? There must be more to this than a simple little campaign to get the vote for women in the Territory of Montana. Now is the time to tell me what this whole caper is really about."

"The vote for women," she said.

"Mrs. Adams . . ." he stopped when she held up her hand.

"Please, call me Libby. Everyone does. May I call you Spur?"

He nodded. "Now, Libby, start relying on your expert. Men in the street were hooting and laughing at your parade, at your try to get the vote. This is not an issue to call for assassination. Not even the governor would send a plea to Washington for that alone. What else is involved?"

"I'm not sure. The man in Virginia City is Rufus Laidlaw. He's the Secretary of State, a powerful office. Virginia City is our capital."

"I've never heard of Virginia City in Montana."

"That's part of the problem, no one has. The state capital should be here in Helena."

"So that's part of this mess. He wants to keep it there and you're working to bring the capital to Helena?"

"A lot of people are working toward that goal, but

they're not getting shot."

"With a move here, land values would skyrocket, right?" Spur demanded. "And businesses already here would grow tremendously. But land values in Virginia City would slump, and the town would end up as a ghost town."

"Yes. But that's not the point of the move. Helena is where the most people in the state live. It's a natural center for trade, transportation, business. The capital should be here."

"What's Laidlaw's stake in Virginia City?"

"He owns a lot of property there. I guess he's afraid he would lose most of his money." She looked up quickly. "But a move of the capital is more important to the state than any one man."

"Or woman, voting or not," Spur said.

"But the vote is still one of my main interests. I have a bill introduced into the legislature in Virginia City to give women over twenty-one the vote. It would change the state constitution to read any legal resident over the age of twenty-one shall have the vote regardless of race, creed or religion. It's been introduced and is now in committee. We hope to have it brought to a vote before the end of the session."

"But it probably doesn't have a chance to pass, right?"

"Probably. But many good ideas have had to be tried a dozen times before they become law. It's the way things work in politics."

"Still this is not a reason to kill you. I understand two railroads are starting to send survey teams out to pick a right of way across the northern states. Would that have anything to do with Helena?"

"We hope so, Spur. If we could get the Northern Pacific to bring their tracks through Helena, it would give our economy a boost just like trains have to other western cities."

Spur rubbed one big hand over his weathered face. "Yes, yes, the old railroad route fight. Now we're getting somewhere. I've seen a dozen small local wars fought over where the tracks should go. And sometimes the survey teams are prone to allow local causes and even bribes to alter their judgement."

"I've heard that, but Helena is the logical route for them, the best grade level. They probably will come west along the Yellowstone River to get the easy grade, then cut northwest through Montana heading for Seattle."

"Then it's the railroad route that this is all about?"

"Partly. If we can get the state capital here, the railroad would be a lot more willing to come this way. We would have everything to offer them. It would be good for the state, good for the railroad and good for Helena."

"And bad for Virginia City."

"True," Libby said. She divided her long hair over her shoulder in three strands and began braiding them, then unbraided them and combed them out.

"What else aren't you telling me, Libby?"

"In a day or two there will be a meeting here in town of the Montana State Legislature Capital Relocation Committee. They'll be looking over the area, checking out where the city says the new capital can be built, talking with residents, generally gathering information about whether or not to move the capital here."

"Which doesn't make Mr. Laidlaw happy. Will you be testifying before the committee?"

"Yes. It's probably one of the most important contributions I can make to Helena. If I live that long."

"You will." Spur watched her. She was beautiful, she was nervous, she was so lovely and vulnerable right then that he wanted to take her in his arms and hold her, tell her that he would let nobody hurt her. But she still held back. There was something she wasn't telling him.

"Libby, what's the other problem? Something else is coming along that you're not telling me about. Right?"

She looked up and her hand came up to her mouth in surprise. Her lovely brown eyes went wide in surprise, and then her face set grimly.

"Yes. I just got word this afternoon. A railway survey crew is working its way toward Helena. They should arrive in a day or two depending on their progress. We think it is significant that they are moving through here with one of their three or four proposed routes."

"Tomorrow or the next day. Them here as well as the relocation committee. Sounds like Mr. Laidlaw will be in town as well, in fact I'd bet he's already here."

"I could check with my hotels."

"You own all four?"

She nodded.

"No, I'll find out. One other problem. You're an important person in this town. You own a lot of property, businesses, control the lives of a lot of employees. Do you know of any of those people who might want to try to shoot you?"

She stared at Spur for a moment. Then slowly shook her head. "No, I don't know of any. I don't think there are any. You see, Spur I came from a poor family. I've lived all my life here in Helena. My father ran a small hardware store for Alexander Adams.

"A kinder, more generous, more gracious man never lived than my late husband. His first wife died in childbirth along with his son. He was a widower for years, then one day he took a fancy to me when I was eighteen. He courted me for a year, then married me, and we had seven beautiful years together.   •

"He taught me everything about business. I can never have children, Spur. We found that out after two years of trying." She laughed. "Lordy, did we try! Then he concentrated on teaching me how to run his business firms so I could carry on when he died. He was forty-one years older than I was, but it didn't matter to us, except this one way. He knew he would never have an heir.

"I've tried to run things the way he would have, or perhaps a little softer, a little easier. The bank has never foreclosed on a loan since I took over. Neither have we ever lost money on a loan.

"In six years I have never fired an employee. We have a way of taking care of our own. One man was a drunk. We talked to him and his family, and spelled out what they all had to do. We helped him, and now he's the manager of my bank. I try to be as fair as I can with all of my fellow workers."

"I've heard that," Spur said. "So we're making progress, ruling out suspects. What about the gold mines? You have two or three I understand."

"Gold isn't as important to this town as it was. We began in a gold rush, true. Four old prospectors were about on their last legs. They decided to make one more try, then give up and go back to honest work. They dug into this ravine with a trickle of

water down it. Those four men called it the Last
Chance Gulch. The gulch runs down what is now
Main Street here in Helena. They hit it big, worked
out the panning, found the mother lode and made
them all rich. Now we've taken out more than ten
million dollars worth of gold around here. The
experts say we have at least that much left, but the
real mining riches will be in other areas, copper,
silver, other minerals."

She stood and he enjoyed watching the way she
moved. "No, Spur, the gold mines are not a factor in
my wounding."

"Which brings us back to Laidlaw, the relocation
committee and the railway right of way."

"Yes. Spur, I want you to stay here in my house,
that will be added protection. We have plenty of
rooms, for goodness sakes. I'll send someone to get
your things out of your room. We'll leave it
registered in your name as a decoy. Might be a good
idea to register at the other three hotels as well."

Spur grinned. "Yes, be glad to stay here. I'm sure
your cook is better than they are at the hotel. You
sure you haven't done detective and law enforce-
ment work before?"

"Just my business training."

Spur stood. "I'd like to make a tour of the saloons.
Find out what I can about what folks are saying, the
gossip, the speculation about who shot you. Bound
to be some talk. Some of it might be helpful. Also, I
want to try to find Mr. Laidlaw."

"Be careful of the man. He's a snake."

An hour later, Spur had sipped beers in four
saloons, and everywhere he found the same feeling
toward Libby Adams. No one had a bad word to say
about her. In two taverns they drank a toast to her
recovery. Spur had never found this sort of feeling

toward the town's rich person anywhere in the west.

A man at the bar next to him began talking about Libby. Spur had not brought up her name.

"Woman is a gem, she's about perfect. Know what she did for the Johnsons? The man of the family got himself killed in a mine shaft. Wasn't even her mine. She paid off the loan on the little house they built. Put the wife to work in one of her stores, and rounded up another widow lady to move in with the Johnsons and take care of the two young uns.

"Know this for damn sure, 'cause the Johnsons is my in-laws. She tries to help out. More than you can say for most rich folks. Don't remember anybody in town going hungry. Libby always sends somebody over with a sack of groceries, a hundred pounds of flour and a sack of spuds."

Spur bought the man a nickel beer and moved on. Libby Adams seemed to be the best liked person in town. He checked at the three other hotels, registered, and said he'd move in later that night. None of them had a Rufus Laidlaw registered.

When he got back to the Adams house, Spur let the solid brass knocker drop and almost at once the maid answered the door. She was about eighteen, barely five feet tall, and fair.

"Evening Mr. McCoy. Your things come and I put them upstairs in the big guest room. Mrs. Adams gone to bed and she said I should show you up to your room."

Spur followed her up the curving staircase to the second floor. The whole house was a showcase. He wondered how much Alexander Adams had spent on it.

The room was nearly twenty feet square, with a huge four poster bed with a canopy, two windows that looked out over the town, a sofa and chair, and a small table, as well as a dresser and writing desk. Over a hundred books showed their bindings in a wall-built bookcase.

"Mrs. Adams said I should lay out your things," the maid said. "My name is Charity."

"Thanks, Charity, but you don't need to bother."

She opened the carpetbag and looked up smiling. "It's really no trouble, and if Mrs. Adams said do it, I must." She put his clothes in the dresser and the carpetbag beside it.

He sat on the sofa chair and watched her. She was small, barely five feet tall, he guessed, but had a fully rounded figure. Her hair was blonde, cut short and he remembered her eyes were blue. She finished with the carpetbag and came and stood in front of him.

"Mr. McCoy, is there anything else I can do for you?"

"Thanks, Charity, you've done plenty."

"I could perhaps help in other ways." She knelt on the floor in front of him and slowly began to unbutton her blouse. Spur noticed that she wore little under it. He could see her nipples straining through the cloth.

"Charity . . . you don't need. . . ."

"I know." She looked up, and smiled. "I thought you might want some relaxation. I give good back-rubs!" Her blouse was open now and it was plain that she wore nothing under it. The sides swung back showing the edges of her breasts.

When Spur sat down his legs had spead and now she moved on her knees between his legs and looked up at him, smiling broadly.

"Mr. McCoy, you're the handsomest man I think I ever seen. I'd be proud to relax you a little . . . just however you need to be relaxed." Her hand came out and rubbed his crotch, where Spur could not stop his hardon from growing. She found it and cried out softly in delight.

She shook off the blouse and her breasts bounced from the movement. They were fuller than Spur guessed, still childless pink areolas with soft brown nipples that had filled with hot blood and enlarged and risen.

She leaned forward and unfastened his belt, then opened the buttons down his pants and spread the fabric. She worked through his short underwear and claimed the prize.

"I found him!" she yelped in delight. "Oh, such a big boy! Him and me gonna get along just fine!" She popped his penis out of his pants and bent at once and kissed the turgid rod. The purple head throbbed and twitched and she giggled.

"Oh, lordy, yes, but him and me gonna do good things for each other!" She bent, kissed his staff again, then opened her mouth and sucked him inside.

Spur's hands reached down for her breasts and toyed with them as she bobbed up and down on him. He caught her head and pulled her up and off him.

"Maybe we should talk about this on the bed. Does the door have a lock?"

Charity darted to the door and locked it, and was back at the bed when he got there. Her eyes sparkled. She reached up and helped him take off his vest, and then his shirt.

"Always wanted to do that," she said. Spur caught her skirt, found the buttons and undid them. She kicked the skirt away and was naked.

"I hoped that you would let me stay," she said. She stepped off the bed and finished undressing him. Then she jumped up on him and wound her legs around his torso.

"Standing up?" Spur said.

"Never have that way," she said. "Is it possible?"

Spur lifted her with one hand around her soft bottom and moved her to one side slightly, then lowered her. His shift slid into her waiting, hot sheath and she yelped in surprise and delight.

"Oh, yes!" She bounced back and forth on his hard pole and made small sounds deep in her throat. Spur watched sweat bead on her forehead as she rode him like a pony. Soon her breath came in short gasps and she began pounding harder and faster.

She erupted into a jolting climax as her whole body shivered in joy and release, then vibrated and shook as spasm after spasm tore through her. She closed her eyes tightly and her face grimaced as she made the joy last as long as it possibly would.

Charity pushed her sweating face against his chest and hugged him tightly, then wiggled in his arms.

"Move down on the bed without letting go of me," she said. "I want you on top of me hard and heavy!"

He made the maneuver and she relaxed. Spur came out of her until only the head of his shaft was in her delicate neither lips, then he drove in hard.

"Oh, damn!" she yelped.

He repeated the movement a dozen times and with each thrust she panted and said "Oh, damn!" He could tell she was building again. Now he concentrated on his own desires and pounded short and hard, driving her soft fanny a foot into the down featherbed as the powering unstoppable surge came and he exploded deep inside her, splashing her with his stored up seed and draining him into the mini-death as he sagged on top of her.

She put her arms around his back, pinning him in place, as she finished her own climax and kissed him hard on the mouth before turning her head to suck in lungsful of new air to replenish her spent body.

Five minutes later she reached up and kissed him.

"Again, lover. Do it again, right now!"

Spur stirred and found he was still erect and began to make love to her again. She looked at him.

"I want to be on top, please?"

He rolled away from her and she sat on his chest a moment, then lowered her breasts one at a time into his eager mouth.

"It feels so good when you do that! Like all the wonderful things in the world all at once! It's like I just want you to be in me and around me and chewing on me and fucking me all the time!"

"How about all night instead?" Spur asked.

"Oh, yes! Anyway you want to. In any place you want!" She pulled her breast from his mouth and moved down. Slowly she came over his turgid, pulsating shaft and guided it into her heartland.

"Just wonderful!" she screeched. "So beautiful! I want to stay just like this all night!" She laughed. "But then the next position I'll want to stay that way all night too!"

She hung over him, rocking back and forth. Spur found her breasts with his hands and held them, massaging them tenderly. Quickly she climaxed, her whole body shaking and bouncing. She growled and whined as the passion blasted through her. Then she was back in her position using him like a rocking horse, moving them both toward the next explosion.

It was nearly midnight when Spur leaned up on an elbow and stroked her cheeks, and throat, then her smooth sleek breasts.

"We should have brought something to eat from

the kitchen," Spur said. She rolled over top of him, bounced off the bed and went to a box that he had not seen in the corner.

"We did! I figured you would be hungry or thirsty." She spread out the food and drinks between them on the bed.

"We have three kinds of hard sausages, two kinds of cheese, lots of crackers, and dill pickles and two bottles of wine and just for emergencies a bottle of whiskey. Anything else that you might want?"

He used the knife she had brought and sliced the hard sausage into slices and put them between crackers along with slices of the dill pickle and then uncorked a bottle of red wine.

They drank and ate the crackers. Charity ate a little, then played with him, teased him and soon she had him back in bed. She pressed his face into her stomach and moved it downward. Spur found where she wanted him to go and his tongue rimmed her nether lips then plunged in and she climaxed at once and screeched in such rapture that Spur had to clamp his hand over her mouth to quiet her.

They came together three more times and Spur shook his head.

"I'm finished, Charity. You outlasted me."

"Seven times is wonderful!" she said, kissing his chest. "Now get some sleep and we can start again in the morning." Spur kissed her breasts, they cleared the bed of the food and drink and softly lay down in each other's arms. Before he dropped off Spur resolved to wake up at five-thirty. He had developed that ability and now used it whenever he needed to.

Charity went to sleep at once. Spur nuzzled her gently, then lay back and let sleep overtake him.

4

Will Walton knew where he was headed. He tried to keep that one fact clear and straight in his thinking. Usually he could, except when the headaches came. Then he went out of his mind. He knew he did. He could remember some of it.

Now he gritted his teeth and rode on. After that bad day in Kansas when he discovered he was officially dead and his "widow" had sold his ranch, things had been a little better.

He knew he had a son!

Will had been naked and without a penny to his name after that day, but he had survived. He had learned well in his wanderings how to survive. By instinct he lived one day at a time. He had taken clothes off a line at night. Walked around the town until he found a horse in front of a saloon after the place had closed.

He stole the animal and rode out of town quickly, used his saddle "O" ring and a pair of pliers to alter the brand on the horse, then traded saddles with another saloon patron and soon no one could identify the horse and saddle.

He had worked north from Kansas.

In North Platte, Nebraska he ran into trouble
again. He had worked for a month at a ranch outside
of town, had nearly twenty dollars in his pocket
when he moved on north and stopped in the general
store in North Platte to buy enough supplies for a
two week ride.

He never could remember what happened after he
had been in the store for a while picking out
supplies. He must have thought he was in the war
again. That's what it always was. He came back to
reality in the local jail and the sheriff had told him
he wounded a man and almost scared the store
owner's wife to death.

"You acted crazy," the sheriff said. "Kept yelling
about Rebels coming, and something about the
Wilderness." The lawman paused, passing in a plate
full of dinner through the bars. It was home cooking
from his wife.

"You were in the war, Walton?"

"Yes sir. First Lt. Will Walton of the Ohio
Twenty-Fifth under Colonel Richardson."

The sheriff rubbed his lean face. "That was one of
the outfits slaughtered in the Wilderness for damn
sure. I barely got out of there with my life. Still got
a minie ball from an old muzzle loader in my hip.
Some Reb was using black powder and a ball that
day."

Will ate the food. He hadn't had a meal that good for
a month, or maybe two months he couldn't remember.
The ranch food had been barely palatable.

"I thank you kindly for the victuals, Sheriff.
What happens now?"

"Where you heading for?"

"Worked out at the Bar S for a month to get a

grubstake. Moving up to Montana to try to find my family. Wife thought I was killed at the Willderness. Damn near was."

"Know how you feel. You had twenty dollars in cash on you when I brought you in. Month's wages all right. Jenny said you was buying trail food. Everything seems to check."

"Figure I can look at the brand book in Montana and see if my brand is up there, the WW. Ain't one registered in Nebraska. One in Kansas is mine, but I ain't there."

"Like to help," the sheriff said. He lifted his right leg off his left and stood with a limp. "You know you shot up the store?"

"God no!" Will blinked back the start of tears. "Damn! Just went crazy. Happened before. Got this slug across the back of my head."

The sheriff unlocked the cell and looked at the scar. He shivered.

"Lucky you ain't dead and buried," the lawman said.

"That's what the Rebs kept telling me. Prisoner of the Confederates for about a month before it ended."

"Expenses, let's see. We got a store window for ten dollars, and ruined merchandise of about five more." The sheriff said it half to himself. "How much you need for grub?"

"I figured five dollars of dried goods and coffee and possibles would do me for near a month."

"Got myself a little fund I use from time to time," the sheriff said. "I'll have a talk with the people concerned."

Will thanked him and rolled on the hard bunk, but he couldn't sleep.

The next morning the sheriff was back at his cell.

"Time to move, Will," the sheriff said.

"Where?"

"North toward Montana, and a bit west."

"How come?" Thought I owed some money, had some charges against me."

"All cleared up. Talked to the wounded man into not pressing any charges. We put it down as drunk and disorderly and I fined you two dollars, plus expenses. They came to twelve dollars for the window and the goods at the store.

"Then it costs you five dollars for that list of grub you wanted at the store. He threw in some extra I think. I took care of most of it from my fund. Which leaves you fifteen dollars pocket change to get you to your next job."

Tears streamed down Will's face.

"Don't know how to thank you . . . Most folks don't look kindly . . . God bless you, Sheriff!"

Will had no idea what brought on his "spells" as he called them. Sometimes he had no recall of how long they lasted. After he got out of jail he remembered working his way into Scotts Bluff, Nebraska and then on to Casper, Wyoming. But then things faded again.

Now he stared around, not sure where he was. He had no understanding at all about what month it was, let alone the year. The last period of time he could remember had been in Nebraska. He sat up on the edge of a small stream. He still had a horse, and some provisions. For that he was thankful.

Casper was somewhere behind him, but where was this? He had little idea which direction to move. For a half hour he sat on the small stream bank and studied the land around him. He was into some mountains, but could see no signs of life. There was no road or trail, no smoke, no railroad, no wagon road, not even a cow grazing on the grass in the valley.

For a moment he thought he heard a shot, then he was sure, two more shots. Pistol, he knew at once and wondered how he was certain.

From the west! He hurried to his horse and rode in that direction up a small slope to the top of the ridge. When he stared down on the other side he saw a cabin with smoke rising from the chimney. Two men with masks over their faces were riding around the cabin, shooting through the windows.

Automatically Will reached for the rifle in the boot and to his surprise found one. He dove to the ground behind cover, levered a round into the chamber and killed one of the attackers with his first shot. The second rider turned, surprised, then began to ride off when Will's second round took him in the shoulder and knocked him from the horse. Will's next rifle slug powered through the robber's chest, killing him instantly.

Will remained where he was, out of sight.

Ten minutes later he heard a screen door hinge squeak and saw the cabin's back door opening. A face peered out.

"Hello out there. I belong here. Don't shoot no more. They was just the two of them."

It was a woman's voice Will figured.

"You all right?" Will asked still concealed.

"Rightly so, now I am. Come on down. Don't want to dig in these two trash all by myself. I ain't got no man no more."

Will lifted from his concealment, took the reins to his horse and walked down the hill.

The woman came out of the cabin. She was older than her voice indicated. Pushing thirty-five, he decided. She wore a gingham dress that covered her neck to wrist to ankles. Brown hair had been done up in a bun at the back of her neck.

He stopped a dozen feet from her.

She looked at him and he could see the disappointment there.

"Thanks. Thanks for saving my life, and Sally's. We're obliged." He hesitated.

"I got to be riding on," Will said quickly. "Just don't like to see nobody get shot at who ain't shooting back."

"Ran out of rounds. Damn polecats knew about it. They was both rawhiders. Knew they was around here someplace."

"Just where is this, ma'am?"

"You don't know?"

"Got myself lost."

"Easy enough. We about twenty miles from the Montana line up in the Bighorn Mountains. Not too far from little place called Sheridan, Wyoming."

"Appreciate it, ma'am. Well, I better be moving on."

"Most evening. You could stay for supper. I would appreciate a hand with the burying, too, if'n you don't mind."

"Oh, yes. I did kill them." He dropped the reins to his horse confident that it wouldn't move more than a few feet to graze. "You have a shovel?"

He kept the revolvers and two rifles the pair had, then gave one of the horses and saddles to the woman, and said he'd take the other and sell it somewhere.

It took him two hours to dig through the rocky soil to put the two rawhiders underground. At that they only had a foot and a half of dirt and rocks over them. But it would be enough to keep the wolves away from them.

When he was finished the woman brought out a cup of hot coffee, and when he tasted it, he smiled.

"Best coffee I had in years," he said.

She smiled. "I got a boiler filled with hot water. You a mind for a good bath and a shave, I won't complain none."

"Bath . . ."

"You could use one. You see I don't go between the blankets with no man without a bath."

"Between . . ."

"Figure I owe you. Them rawhiders was telling me what they would do to me and Sally, and she not fourteen yet. So you get inside and Sally will scrub your back if you have a mind to. I'll be along soon as I feed the chickens. We'll have a late supper and then you stay the night. Lite out first thing with sunrise if you want. Figure I owe you."

"Well now . . ."

"You don't want me, just say. Reckon you could have Sally, even though she ain't been spoiled yet."

"Not, not that at all. Just been so long. I mean a real lady and all."

"No different last time I heard. A woman is a woman." She smiled. "Fact is, I'd enjoy you staying over. Been three years since my husband died . . ."

Will went inside, found Sally, a miniature of her mother and well developed fourteen, a grown woman already. She helped him fill the round white cedar bath tub then he shooed her out and stripped off his clothes. He was grimy. He washed for a half hour then heard the door open.

"My name is Shirley, it matters any."

She walked in front of him where he sat cross legged in the tub. He made no move to hide himself.

"Wish there was room in there for me." She smiled. "I sent Sally to the long well. We got time."

As he scrubbed once more, she slowly undressed until she stood naked before her. She watched with satisfaction as his penis progressed from limpness to a stiff erection jutting out of the water.

She bent over the tub. "Wash my tities so they'll taste better."

He did, then she stood as he did and she dried him with a towel and led him through a curtain to her bedroom.

"No man's slept in here for three years," she said. "Hope to hell you are good in bed."

"Everybody is good in bed," Will said and they rolled onto the blankets spread over a straw mattress.

"Oh, damn!" she said and laughed.

"What?"

"Your shave. You'll get that right after the third go round in bed here. I got a powerful need to be filled."

The next morning, Will sat on the bed. He had dressed and started out into the rest of the cabin when he heard the girl. She was asking her mother what it felt like to be poked with a man's long "thing."

Shirley just laughed and said Sally would find out some day.

When he came out they both laughed and he grinned and hadn't felt so good in months.

Over breakfast she suggested it. "No sense you moving on. Got yourself a ready made family. Preacher comes around once a month. He could do the marrying. Sally needs a Pa. The ranch here ain't much, but a man could make it pay. I got three hundred head of cattle somewhere in the hills."

Will told them about his quest.

"So I'm still married and I have to find my family.

They could be in Montana."

Shirley scowled. "Most likely they ain't. Wasn't in Wyoming or Nebraska or Kansas. You got Texas and Arkansa and Nevada and about twenty more states and territories. You aim to try them all?"

"If I have to," Will said softly.

Sally laughed. "I don't think he liked the way you did him, Ma," the girl said. "Let me try."

Mother slapped daughter and spun her around. "You mind your tongue, girl!"

She shook her head. "I know how you men are. You get something in your craw and you got to go find it. Gold or silver, or a new ranch or an old wife. I know.

"My man didn't die, he ran off for gold somewhere. I figure he got himself killed because of his quick temper. He ain't coming back. I got to fend for myself. You want one more try on the bed, just to be sure you don't like it here?"

"Shirley, you were remarkable, delightful. But it's a matter of conscience. I must find my son. I must know what happened to them."

She did lure him to the bed again, and this time neither of them bothered to tell Sally to go away so she stood by the bed watching it all with youthful delight as her hand under her dress rubbed at her crotch.

He left an hour later, clean shaven, with three sets of pants and clean shirts in his kit bag. They were a little large for him, but Shirley said her husband would never need them. She packed him enough cooked food to last two days and cried when he left.

He rode north and east for Sheridan the way she told him. Before noon the headache came again. Just before he found Sheridan, he was back in the Wilderness firing at the Rebels as they stormed through the brush. He left his horse and charged away to the rear with the rest of the blue coats, and ran until he fell from exhaustion.

When he came back to reality all he had was an empty six-gun in his hand and the clothes on his back. He had no idea how to find his horses, his food or his clean clothes.

With a futile sigh, Will tried to blink away the headache as he walked toward a smoke to the north. It should be some town. He couldn't remember the name of it, and he wasn't sure even what state this was.

One thing he remembered. His name was Will Walton and he was heading for Montana. Exactly why, he wasn't sure.

5

The next morning, Spur's mental alarm clock misfired and he slept in. Libby was up and off to her office in the bank by 7:30. It was her normal work time and she went over various reports and made some business decisions just the way Alexander had trained her to do years before.

She sat back in her big chair and looked out the second story window of the bank and down the tree shaded main street. This was a great little town, and she was going to put it on the map and make it the capital of Montana! It was logical, reasonable, and Alexander would have wanted it that way. She had been in the fight from the first three years ago for the move to Helena.

She looked at a scale map of the town's business district which she had specially prepared. Each of the blocks was represented with the individual stores and houses showing. Those she owned were shaded in light blue for residences and light pink for businesses. She had twenty-one retail firms along the three blocks of Main Street and twenty rental houses she had brought over the years.

Not bad. She had picked up six new commercial operations since Alexander died. They were logical acquisitions to get rid of competition or to open a new venture. Things were progressing well. But she was disturbed about one thing.

She was only thirty-two years old, and already she was thinking about what had bothered Alexander for many years. She had no heir. Who would carry on after she was gone? It was a fact that she should think about. She could not marry some young man and have an heir, the way Alexander hoped he could. She would give a hundred thousand dollars if she could bear a child!

She could always adopt. Usually a single woman could not adopt, but with her resources and contacts she could probably make it work for her. She put the problem out of her mind. Her secretary knocked on the door and came in.

Mrs. Unruh was almost forty, wrote the most beautiful hand of anyone Libby had ever seen, and was a highly organized and efficient person.

"Hal Barnes is here, Mrs. Adams. He's with the hardware store, lost his wife few months back."

Libby's frown faded. "Yes, bring us some coffee and send him in."

The man who came in her office was slight, his shoulders stooped and he had a look of intense concern on his pale face.

"Sit down, Hal. I thought it was time we had a little talk." He looked up with a worried expression. She hurried on. "Hal, the hardware store has been doing well these past few months. New construction is up in town and that always helps, but the hardware business is a problem solving service. People tell me you're the best problem solver in town."

Hal looked up, a smile creased his face, then vanished.

"Thank you, Mrs. Adams."

"Hal, your total sales are up and so is the profit on the store. You're doing just remarkably well. I'm arranging a bonus for you at the end of the month over your usual profit percentage."

"Oh, really? Well, thank you, Mrs. Adams. I appreciate it." The smile stayed this time, his shoulders came back a little and he sat up straighter.

"Hal, we were all shocked and saddened by your loss. Emmy was a wonderful woman and we all miss her. I have been concerned about you these last two months. I know it's been hard. I've been through the tragedy of having a spouse die, Hal, I understand."

Hal looked at the floor, his shoulders slumping again.

"Hal, I also know that there is a time for grieving, and a time to stop. I think you're at the stopping point, Hal, it's time to do something else other than throw yourself into your work. I appreciate your diligence, but I have another problem I want you to help me with."

Hal looked up, a small frown building on his face.

"You remember Ken Farley. He passed away about six months ago. He worked in one of the mines, a foreman and a good man. His widow has been having a difficult time since then trying to support herself and the two youngsters. Usually I'm not much of a matchmaker, Hal, but I've seen her watching you in church lately on almost every Sunday morning.

"Hal, I think Marie Farley would be pleased if you would call on her now and then. She's a fine woman, but she has her needs, just the way you do."

"But, but she's so pretty . . ."

"Hal, pretty doesn't do a woman a bit of good when she has to go to bed alone every night. You understand what lonely is, I know for sure. I'd be more than pleased if you'd consider calling on Marie. If nothing happens, what have you lost?"

"She wouldn't laugh at me?" Hal asked.

"Hal, you're a fine looking man. You have a good position and are earning more money than half the men in town. From what I've seen of her watching you in church, I think she'd be delighted to have you come calling. After that, see what happens. You might be surprised."

Hal stood taller. His shoulders came back and a smile lit his face like she hadn't seen since his wife died.

"Much obliged for the suggestion, Mrs. Adams. And thank you for the kind words about the store. Gonna make that the best dang hardware store in the state!" He started for the door but turned. "Thanks for the hint about Marie. She comes in the store once in a while." He grinned. "Think I might go up to her place right now and see if there's any handyman jobs I can do for her around that big house of hers. Must be something, no man being there for six months now." He nodded and smiled.

"Thank you, Hal," Libby said a broad grin on her face.

Mrs. Unruh came to the door when Hal had left. "Your only other business this morning is Orville. He's from the livery stable."

Libby frowned. "Yes, ask him to come in."

Libby stood with her back to the window on a foot high platform so she would not have to look up at the man. He would have to squint to see her against the light. In this case everything she could do to help her commanding management position would be a plus.

Orville walked in wearing his stable clothes, dirty jeans, boots, a shirt with sleeves torn off at the elbows, and a grimy hat he twisted in his hands. He was about thirty, unwashed and irreverent. He had a half sneer on his face as he stopped in front of her desk.

"Yes, ma'am?"

"Orville, Greg says you've been stealing money from the cash box at the livery stable. Is that true?"

"Hell no! Pardon me, Ma'am. I ain't stole nothing."

"Very well, Orville. I guess I'll have to turn it over to Sheriff Palmer. He'll arrest you for grand theft and put you in jail until the trial. You'll need a lawyer, of course. Can you hire one? They ask for half their fee in advance. Most charge only twenty dollars a day."

Orville stared at her. "Twenty . . . Hell I only borrowed thirty dollars. . . ."

"Orville, you're changing your story?"

He sighed, his hat turned faster. "Yeah. I guess so. Don't want to go to jail. Greg really signed a paper against me?"

"He did. I told him to. He says you've been stealing a dollar a day, and he told you to stop five or six times."

"Like to gamble a little after work. Nothing else to do. But even on the nickel table it takes money."

"So you admit you stole from the livery?"

"Yes, ma'am."

"Orville, do you know in six years I've never fired anyone who works for any of my businesses?"

"Heard that, yes ma'am."

"I could break my record with you. Is that what

you want?''

"No ma'am."

She sighed and looked out the window. How did she get to be a judge and jury here? She turned back. "Orville, exactly how much did you take from the cash box?''

"Thirty-four dollars. I kept track. I was gonna win big and pay it all back. I . . .''

She held up her hand. "Orville, you can keep working at the livery but you're going to have to do a few things. First, you'll be docked two dollars a week from your pay until the thirty-four dollars are repaid. Is that perfectly understood?''

"Jeeeze . . only make four dollars a week. That cuts me to two dollars . . .''

"Think hard before you steal again. It's only for seventeen weeks. Second, Orville you must promise never to steal from the livery again. If you do, I'll have you arrested and tried. Is that understood?''

"Yes, ma'am.''

"Third, you are not to gamble ever again. No more cards or dice or faro. Nothing.''

"But . . . no cards?''

"Play for matches, it's just as much fun.''

"Damn! . . . all right.''

"Can you read, Orville?''

"No ma'am, just never had the chance.''

"You will now. You are to wash up good, put on clean clothes and report to Mrs. Unruh in the outer office every week day morning at seven-thirty for an hour of reading lessons. When Mrs. Unruh is satisfied that you are literate, you can stop coming.''

"No . . . Not a chance. I . . . I'd feel silly.''

"Orville, how old are you?''

"Twenty-two.''

"Lots of time yet for you. After you learn to read and get a haircut and shave regularly, I might be able to find a better job for you, something that would pay in relation to your new knowledge and ability."

Orville frowned. "Pay more? Maybe in two or three weeks?"

"No. First you repay the $34. And you finish learning to read. Maybe three months."

"Maybe ten dollars a week?"

She smiled. It was a fortune to him. "That's possible, Orville. Now get cleaned up before you go back to the stable. Shave every day, and come tomorrow morning for your reading lesson."

"Yes, ma'am." He paused. "Appreciate this, Mrs. Adams, only don't tell nobody about the readin'." He turned and hurried out of the room.

Spur McCoy came into her office before the door closed. She looked up and smiled. A stab went through her. She sat down behind the desk and felt her knees give way. Almost at once there was a burning between her legs and she was wet down there. She took a slow, nervous breath and tried to control her voice.

"My most difficult caller all morning," she said. "Sleep well?" She tried to sound normal, but already her breath was coming faster. Damn it!

He evidently saw no hidden meaning in her words. Spur sat down in a chair next to the big desk.

"Matter of fact I slept extremely well. That bed is better than the ones in your hotels."

"That's true. Seen the sheriff yet?"

"On my way. Just got outside of that big breakfast that Charity brought me."

"Glad you liked it." He had liked Charity well last night too, she knew. God, could she keep up this front?

"I have a couple of questions."

She watched him, waiting.

"Is Laidlaw the main person who would suffer if the state capital moved here?"

"No. Most of the merchants in Virginia City would eventually have to close up and move. There isn't enough basic work or any industry there for the people."

"Is the Yellowstone River the most logical route for the rail line through Montana?"

"Absolutely. They can use the river bed for a gradual grade and through natural passes for over four hundred miles. There hasn't been an easy grade like that anywhere else in the West for any of the railroads. It's a hundred times out a hundred that the engineers and grade surveyors will pick that route."

"Just wanted to make sure. Looks like Laidlaw is fighting against a stacked deck."

"But he's still going to fight. I know the man. He is not a good person."

"A good man is hard to find these days."

"I know," Libby said with a big grin. For one wild second she almost jumped up and pulled open her bodice. Instead she laughed to cover up her emotion. "I've been hunting one. They all want my money. How about you?"

"I'm not interested in money. I've been in that situation and walked away from it."

Her brows lifted. "You'll have to tell me about it sometime."

"Glad to. A reminder for you and your safe-keeping. No public speaking engagements, and no damn parades."

She laughed and nodded.

"Now, I have to go see the sheriff about a man in jail."

Libby watched him go and a strange feeling seeped through her. She had not felt anything like that in a long, long time. She knew at once what it was, raw, animal desire, sexual wanting and so strong that she knew she was damp and a burning came between her legs again.

The feeling was so intense that she cried out, and Mrs. Unruh hurried into her office.

"Yes, Mrs. Adams?"

"Oh, no, Mrs. Unruh, I changed my mind, not right now, please. Do I have any more appointments this morning?"

"No ma'am."

"Thank you, please don't disturb me for a while. Thank you."

The door closed and she was alone. Libby had forced herself not to think about the night her husband died. Now that was all she could think about. It had been wonderful.

Alexander Adams was a talented, tender lover. He had responded to her sleek young, firm, energetic body like a teenager. They made love every other night and couldn't wait to get to it.

On the night he . . . died, he had been more anxious than usual. They had a lovely dinner, then bathed each other in the big specially built bathtub, and luxuriated on the feather bed. The second time they made love he said he felt a pain in his chest, but he decided it was only stomach gas.

An hour later in the middle of the third love-making he had screamed and died of a massive heart attack just before he could climax.

She had been frantic. Somehow she knew he was dead even as she dressed and had one of the servants run for the doctor.

Since then she had not known any man.

Sex!

She had put it entirely out of her mind. She had concentrated on what Alexander had trained her to do. She ran his companies with such efficiency and drive that they became even more prosperous. She had no time for sex. There was no overpowering need. Once or twice her "happy fingers" had snuggled between her legs and rubbed herself to ecstasy, but that had ended after the first month or two.

During the past six years many men had wooed her. Some had been subtle, some blatant, one almost raped her before she hit him with a lamp. But she had not *needed sex*. That was before yesterday. Before Spur McCoy had lifted her from the dust of the street. He had *touched her!* She had thought of little else since then. Last night she had planned on seducing him, but after dinner she had made excuses to get away from him.

She had been as shy and frightened as a virgin!

So she had sent Charity to him, with instructions to take care of his sexual needs and to be sure to stay all night. That morning Charity had told her in the minutest detail everything they had done in bed the night before.

It had taken all of her willpower to come to the bank this morning. One part of her wanted to dash into his room and waken him and tear all of her clothes off for him. But six years of celibacy had conditioned her. She had come to work.

When he stopped by, she had been moist and flushed in an instant. What was happening to her? She was acting like a fourteen year old who suddenly discovered that sex must be glorious if only some man would show her.

Libby looked down and one hand had curled inside her dress and was rubbing her breast through a tight wrapper.

What in the world?

She pulled her hand away. She had to keep busy. Libby knew that Spur McCoy had work to do, he had to keep her alive. Maybe tonight she could . . . talk to him again. Perhaps he would be interested enough to . . . kiss her.

Her mind surged ahead from the kiss to his fondling and then the foreplay and the undressing and . . .

"Mrs. Adams."

The voice came again, and slowly Libby turned her chair from where she had been staring unseeing out the big window to find Mrs. Unruh standing at her desk.

"Yes, Mrs. Unruh?"

"There's a man here to see you about that parcel of land you wanted to talk about on the north side of town. He says he's interested in selling, but says it has to be today because of a death in his family back East. He will be taking the stage out day after tomorrow, early."

"Yes, Mrs. Unruh. Please ask him to come in. Then send someone over to bring in Mr. Leslie. We may need the lawyer." She would do it, she would throw herself into her work again . . . today. Tonight was going to be a different matter!

6

Spur left Libby's second floor bank building office and walked straight to the jail in the small courthouse. Sheriff Josiah Palmer was finishing his breakfast, and pushed away the tray.

"Figure you want to talk to our prisoner again," Palmer said. Spur said he did and together they went back to the cell.

"Keep him outa here!" the prisoner bellowed. "He's the guy who shot me and tortured me."

"You're breaking my heart," Sheriff Palmer said.

"What else does Rufus Laidlaw have planned for Helena and for Libby Adams," Spur asked.

The man with the two bullet holes in his shoulder now wrapped in bandages shook his head.

"Don't know what the hell what you're talking about. Just told me to discourage McCoy there from staying in town long. Nobody tried to kill McCoy. Scare him, that's all we was trying to do."

"Who taught you to make a grapeshot grenade that way?" Spur demanded.

"Hell, we made them almost like that in the war.

70

Get a newspaper and roll it into an inch wide tube. Fold over the bottom, fill her with black gunpowder and wrap the nails around the outside. One about a foot long used to make just one hell of a hole in a company of Rebs.''

"Never heard of doing that in my outfit," Spur said.

"Maybe you was never short on cartridges and long on powder," the prisoner said. "Hell, Sheriff, we was just trying to scare him. Nobody hurt him. What's the charges for?''

"Attempted murder, assault with a deadly weapon, and using blasting powder in the city limits," Sheriff Palmer said. "Maybe I can think of a couple more. Circuit judge should be through here in about a month."

"I got to stay here for a month?"

"About the size of it. Judge Poindexter just went through on the stage last week. We didn't have no business for him to do."

Outside in the sheriff's private office, the lawman shook his head. "Not much chance this Laidlaw is going to show up and bail him out. I've heard of Laidlaw. He's a man who rides just inside the law, when somebody is watching him."

"He's tied in, that's for damn sure."

Shots sounded down the street.

"What the hell?" the sheriff asked. "Too early in the day for drunk miners. Better see what's going on."

Spur followed him out the door. Half a block down the street a dozen miners and farmers were in the street outside the Golden Nugget saloon. People stood gawking at a fight of some kind.

The two lawmen ran up to the crowd and pushed their way through.

Bud Stoner saw the sheriff and waved. "All over, Sheriff. Damn Yahoo over there shot up my brand new mirror behind the bar, the six-footer I ordered from Chicago. Crazier than a hoot owl, that one is. Claimed the Rebs was charging at him through the thorn bushes and the saplings."

Spur looked where Stoner pointed. A man in tattered clothes crouched behind a horse trough. He had lost his hat and his hair was dirty strings around his shoulders. He had a shaggy beard and farmer shoes. Slowly he edged out from behind the trough, held his hand like a six-gun and "shot" by bending his thumb.

"Bang, bang, bang! Got you, you dirty Reb! Back this way, men, to the rear, fall back. Not a damn chance in hell we can hold off that many Rebels!"

"Crazy is right," Sheriff Palmer said.

Spur put his hand on the lawman's shoulder. "Let me talk to him. Sounds like he had more of the war than he could handle. Yes, I know it's been over for five years, but some men cave in long after the shooting stops. I'll talk to him."

Spur saw the people move back from the man where he cowered behind the trough. He looked like he could be about thirty years old. Spur crouched at the other end of the trough.

"Sergeant, how many men did you lose?" Spur said in a sharp tone. The man behind the planks ignored him, "shooting" his imaginary gun at the crowd of people.

Spur changed the rank. "Lieutenant! I need a casualty report, right now!" Spur snapped. The man behind the trough looked at him.

"Yes, sir! We've had twenty of forty killed, at least ten more wounded who can't move. We had to leave them. Got overrun, the poor bastards. I've got one sergeant and five men left ready to fight."

"Good. What's your name, Lieutenant?"

"Walton, Sir, C company of Colonel Richardson's 25th Ohio. Afraid we're not much of a force to help you fight, Captain."

"Have your men fall in behind you and follow me. We'll get out of this area, too damn many Reb snipers slipping in. Let's move, Lieutenant!"

"Yes sir," Walton said. He stood, slung an imaginary rifle. "Fall in by twos, on me, moving out. Look sharp for Reb snipers!"

Spur turned and walked through the crowd to the closest alley and went down half way along an old brick building. He had no doubt that Walton would follow. The clumping shoes across the boardwalk proved it. When they were out of sight of the crowd, Spur stopped and turned. There was something vaguely familiar about the man's face.

"Your first name, soldier?" Spur demanded.

The bearded man snapped to attention, saluted. "First Lieutenant William Walton, sir."

"You say that's all that's left of Charlie company of the Ohio 25th Regiment?"

"Yes sir. They come through the Wilderness at us, sir. Colonel said nobody could get through there. Right through them bramble bushes that could tear the uniform right off a man. But they come, thousands of them. Blew our picket line right back into the road and across it.

"Heard Stonewall Jackson used twenty-five thousand men in that advance. Smashed us, sir. Cut us into ribbons. Lost all but five of my company."

"Then Spur knew. He had been with the Ohio 25th under Colonel Richardson before they got hit at the Wilderness, just outside of Chancellorsville. He had seen Lt. Walton at Regimental meetings.

"Walton, I'm Captain McCoy, with Baker company. I remember you. I was transferred out a short time before Chancellorsville. But that's all over now. The Reb's are a long ways off now."

Somebody came down the alley, and when Spur turned the man threw a bucket of water at Walton. It hit him in the chest and splashed into his face with a shocking suddenness.

Spur drew and sent a .44 slug winging over the man's head who ran like he was mule kicked out the alley.

When he turned, Will Walton was himself again. He looked at his soaked clothes, then at Spur.

"Must have done it again, right? Acted like I was back in the war. Hope I didn't hurt nobody." He reached for his weapon but found his holster empty. "What happened?"

Spur watched him a moment. "Remember me, Walton? Captain McCoy of Baker company, Ohio 25th."

Walton screwed up his face, squinted, then wiped the water out of his eyes and looked again.

"By damn, it is you, McCoy. Little heavier, more face hair, but the same man." He looked at his ripped cotton flannel plaid shirt and pants too big for him over farmer shoes. "Things been bad for me since the war. Got wounded."

"Let's talk about it, Walton. I'll get a couple of bottles of beer and we'll find some shade and talk."

Ten minutes later they sat under some trees at the edge of town by a little stream.

"Somebody told me this is 1870 already," Walton said. "That's right?"

"True, Will. War's been over for five years."

"By damn! Seems like yesterday. Picked up a head wound there at the end of the Wilderness, then later on I got myself captured by the Rebs. But the war was over soon after. Didn't feel none too good after that Rebel ball sliced through my noodle."

"Been a long time since the war," Spur said.

Walton tipped the beer, then stared at Spur. "Yeah, I remember you now. B company Ohio 25th. Part of Major General Oliver Otis Howard's XI Army Corps. We all got the hell beat out of us down at the Wilderness."

"Didn't you go back to that ranch in Kansas you were always talking about?"

Walton's eyes glazed a minute, then he shook his head. "Oh, yeah, I went back. Nigh on to five years after the war. About two three months ago. Met some Jasper I never seen before. Said he owned my spread. My WW brand was his. Had a bill of sale, and the grant deed signed over by my wife. He said my widow. She thought I got war-killed and sold out and moved."

"Where did she move to, Will?"

"Hell, he didn't know. Nobody knew. I been trying to find my wife. Guy told me I got a son, five or six year old. I got to find my family, McCoy!"

"Did they take the brand with them? The guy in Kansas, was he running your brand on his stock?"

"Nope, guess they must have taken it. Brands. Yeah." He stopped and held his head with both hands. For a minute a high whining sound came from Walton, then he shook his head and looked back at Spur.

"Yeah, the Stockman's brand book. Checked it in Kansas, but no WW. Checked Nebraska and Texas. Missed Wyoming but got a look at the Montana one. There's a WW listed, here near Helena somewhere."

"And you plan to ride out to the ranch and see

who owns it?'' Spur asked.

"Figured to."

Spur looked up and saw the sheriff standing in the edge of the shade.

"First, Will, I better talk to the sheriff. Be right back. He went up to the lawman.

"How much does the barman want for the mirror?"

"Twenty-five dollars. Had it shipped in from Chicago."

Spur gave the sheriff the money. "Any other charges?"

"Not if you take care of him. Don't figure he's dangerous. You say this is all some kind of a throwback to the war?"

"Yes. Some men saw too much killing, did too much blood letting. I've seen it happen in the middle of a battle. One man stood up and began singing a lullaby to his baby daughter. Before we could get him down he was hit with ten bullets."

"Take care of him," the sheriff said and walked away.

Spur intended to. An hour later he had Walton in one of his hotel rooms. He arranged for a bath and went and bought some new clothes for Will. Then they stopped by at a barber shop where Will had his beard shaved off and a proper haircut.

He stood outside the general store looking at himself in the window.

"Sakes! I peer to be about twenty years younger! Don't know why I never shaved it off before. Too dang much trouble, I reckon. You find out where this WW ranch is?"

"Nope, figured you'd want to do that yourself. First, it's time to get some good food into that shrunken belly of yours."

They went to the Bakery Cafe and Spur enjoyed watching Will eat. He began with six hotcakes the size of a dinner plate, four eggs and six slices of bacon. By then it was almost noon so he had a steak and a bowl of chili.

"You ended the war as a prisoner of the Rebels?" Spur asked.

"Yep. Only about two months, but longest damn two months of my life. Rebs didn't have no way to treat the crease on my head. I was out of my mind for about half the time. Lucky they didn't shoot me or let me starve."

"But you came through the Wilderness," Spur said. "We had a lot of generals who didn't know what was happening that day."

"That's not lying at all," Will said. He stared at a man who just came in the cafe door and suddenly he crouched beside his chair.

"They're acoming again, men! Make your shots count!" Lt. Walton checked his line again. Forty men were dug in facing the Wilderness. Nothing but thorn bushes and saplings out ahead them. Everyone said no man in his right mind would attack through there.

But he knew they were coming. He could *smell them!* They were out there.

"Look smart now, lads. Fire and load, fire and load. Keep up the order."

Twenty rifle shots roared fifty feet below them, then directly ahead he saw the gray uniforms. He was calm. It hadn't been this way before.

"Fire when you have a target men!" he shouted, aiming his pistol.

The first rounds from the enemy slammed through the thicket. One caught Private Golloway in the jaw and tore half of his face away. He flopped at Lt. Walton's feet, his one good eye pleading with his commander to help him.

All Will Walton could do was push him aside, flop on the ground behind a log and fire around the end at the blur of gray uniforms working through the brambles. Then the bullets sang around him like hornets.

He saw another man go down, dead without a sound. On the other side of him Corporal Schmidt lifted over the log to fire, but before he could, two Rebel rounds slammed into him. One powered through his forehead, blowing the back of his skull off, showering Lt. Walton with fragments of bone and splatters of brain tissue and rich warm blood.

Lt. Walton screamed and emptied his pistol, then picked up a rifle and saw that it had not been fired and aimed at a running soldier and triggered it. He saw the round jolt into the man, tear through his ear and come out his left eye, throwing the lifeless corpse against a pair of saplings which held it a moment, then it slid to the ground.

Will shook his head and looked at his line. Ten of them were dead. Half the rest wounded. The gray tide of men ran forward, less than five yards from his picket line. There were two hundred infantrymen in front of his forty!

"Pull back, men!" Lt. Walton bellowed over the sound of gunfire. Then the grenadiers ran up and threw their bombs and he saw another of his men die, this one blown in half by the explosion.

"Pull back, damnit!" he roared, but by then there were only a handful of his men could move. They crawled away from the picket line and darted to the rear. Lt. Walton found another rifle and he fired it at the howling horde, then dropped the useless weapon and ran as fast as he could.

He lost track of his men in the brush. The saplings slowed him, the thorn brush clawed at his uniform.

Lt. Walton paused beside a tree to get his breath. A Rebel corporal came around the tree and the men stared at each other for a second in total surprise. The Rebel dug for his pistol. Lt. Walton jerked a knife from his belt and slashed at the enemy's throat. He only nicked his shoulder.

Before the Confederate could upholster his pistol, Lt. Walton had lunged forward, slashed again, cutting across the man's neck deeply. Will jerked the knife back and thrust forward with all his weight behind it at the Rebel's chest. The knife pierced cloth and skin, broke a rib and drove deeply into the dying man's heart.

They both fell to the ground where the Rebel flopped like a straw doll. Will rolled over and reached for the knife sticking from the corpse's chest. He stared at the blood, then heard a rasping wheeze as the final gush of air came from the dead man's lungs.

Will grabbed the knife and ran. For a moment he had no idea which way to move. Then he heard firing in front of him and he turned and ran the other way. He came to a road and found hundreds of tattered, wounded Yanks streaming north. He joined them, then heard the cannon fire behind him and darted into the edge of the thick woods for protection.

Lt. Walton still held the bloody, four-inch knife in his hand. Only then did he notice that his hand and arm were spattered with blood. The left sleeve to his shirt was gone, ripped off somewhere on a thorn bush.

He stopped. The surge of blue shirts kept moving north up the post road. He couldn't take another step. His leg ached and burned. He looked down and saw blood. He had been shot in the leg and never even knew it.

Will slumped beside a tree, his eyes closed.

Later he shook his head. Had he slept? It seemed so quiet. He could see the road but it was empty now. Darkness was coming fast.

Behind him! Someone was coming. He crouched in back of the log, waiting. Someone working through the brush, quietly, a scout? He peered over the fallen log. A gray blur of a Rebel surged toward him. In a reflex action, Will thrust up the bloody blade and saw it drive into the man's chest.

The gray uniform rolled over him and fell to the ground. Will's blade came free. He lifted it ready to strike. The body rolled and he saw the face.

It was a boy, no more than fourteen! He had no weapon. The knife had wounded him high in the shoulder. He bled.

The boy was blond and frightened. He stared at Will for a minute.

"You gonna kill me?" the youth asked.

"Don't know. Where you going?"

"Scouting for General Jackson. Used to live nearby. Know the woods. He sent me."

'How far back is he?"

"Maybe a mile. Front line is about three hundred yards trying to get organized. Advanced too fast."

"You're my prisoner. Stand up, I'll take you to the rear and you'll be questioned, then we'll patch up that shoulder."

Will was on his feet at once. All memory of his wound gone, just the prisoner and his knife. He needed a better weapon. The road, he would be able to find one on the road.

He prodded the boy out of the brush to the dirt trail, found an abandoned rifle that was still loaded and marched his prisoner down the line.

They came around a small bend and before Will could call out, he saw three blue coated troops aim in the dusk and fire at the Rebel uniform. All three bullets crashed into the boy and flung him backward.

Will darted into the brush and the safety of the cover. Damn them! Why had they shot so fast? The Reb had just been a boy! Tears splashed down his cheeks as he ran north. He had to get back beyond the front lines, wherever they were, he had to.

His leg ached now. He limped and used the rifle as a crutch. Why did the boy have to die? He could have been a useful prisoner.

Will stumbled on, then his leg hurt so much he couldn't stand to put any pressure on it at all. He slumped down behind a log and rested. He'd go on in a minute. Just a short rest.

He felt strong hands on his shoulders, then a voice.

"Will. Will Walton, it's all right. They are gone. The war is over, Will. It's all right. You can stand up now, Will. The war is over, you're safe. The killing is over, Will."

Will Walton blinked, stared at the cafe, and at people around watching him. Strong hands urged him to sit down at a table and he did.

Slowly he remembered. He looked at the man who sat across from him.

"God, McCoy, did I do it again? Was I out of my head again? When is it going to stop?"

Spur shook his head. "We don't know, Will. The war did strange things to people. I've seen men run screaming from their first taste of combat. I've seen men who swore they would be cowards turn into the best fighting men I had. The human mind is a strange duck we dont know much about yet. Maybe in a hundred years the doctors will figure us out."

"I was there again, McCoy. It was the Wilderness all over again, the same damn thing. We're on the picket line and the damn Rebs overrun us and we retreat and I come away with only one or two men out of forty. It's horrible."

"Relax, Will. The war is over. You just had a square meal and this afternoon you're going to find out if the WW brand has anything to do with the WW brand you registered down in Kansas. I'll get your six-gun back from the barkeep at that saloon. You'll need some protection riding around here. Just no more shooting up bar mirrors. My expenses can't cover another one."

7

Rufus Laidlaw sat at the back of the Golden Nugget saloon in Helena brooding over a bottle of whiskey. He had downed three shot glasses full already and another sat in front of him waiting.

He knew he shouldn't be here. It was a risk, a gamble. But where the hell would he be today if it hadn't been for some of the risks he had taken?

He picked up the shot glass, then put it down. He knew some people in Helena, but most of them were back in Virginia City. Nobody would recognize him. He tugged the low crowned hat lower over his eyes.

Damn! How could everything go wrong all at once? He had seen the dimwit shoot Libby Adams in the arm. The arm for Christ's sake! How could the asshole have done that? Then he sent the same man and a partner after the Jasper who picked her out of the dust, and one of those men was killed and the other one wound up in jail probably screaming his head off. Laidlaw knew the big man was a whole lot of trouble.

Now he found out that the big stranger who just

got off the stage when Libby was shot was a United
States lawman of some kind. What was he doing
here?

Laidlaw lifted the shot glass and poured the drink
down his throat. It burned. Good. He was feeling too
bad to feel good. The State Capital Relocation
Committee would be here tomorrow or the next day,
and he was sure now that the Helena mayor, a
committee he appointed as well as Libby Adams
would all testify about the glories of bringing the
state capital to Helena. Damn them! What else
could he do?

Just before Montana became a Territory, he had
bought up all the land he could around Virginia
City. If the seat of the territorial government
moved, he would again be living off only his
territorial salary.

His hand was steady as Laidlaw poured the shot
glass full again.

He came to this saloon because it was one of the
few in town that Libby didn't own. He was sleeping
in her hotel under an assumed name. He ate at the
best restaurant in town even though she did own it.

"Damn her eyes!" he muttered and stared at the
whiskey bottle. He'd meet the committee members
whenever they got to town and provide them liquid
and female refreshment for them. Couldn't hurt.

If they decided to move the capital to Helena, that
would just about make it certain that the railroad
would come here too. Shit! Then Virginia City would
be a way station on a stage line that sent a coach
through there once a month!

Laidlaw was a big man, six feet tall and half that
wide. He weighed well over two hundred-eighty
pounds. The only place he could weigh himself was
at the feed store on the big scales that went up to

five hundred pounds. Once or twice a year he went down after the store closed and paid the clerk to let him in and give him the bad news.

His face was fat and pinkish. He shaved meticulously every morning and kept his hair short and sideburns cut short and close above his ears.

Still his eyes seemed lost in the flesh, but burned brightly with a soft green tint. His nose had been mistreated when he was young, usually over arguments about his weight which resulted in fist fights which he almost always lost.

Laidlaw pushed back from the table and headed for the outhouse in the alley. Once out the back door he found the small structure, but realized the door was too small for him to enter. He utilized the side of the outhouse for a splash panel and completed his business there.

Laidlaw wandered out the alley to the street and went down to the Montana Hotel where he entered by the side door. His room was two in on the ground floor. He hated steps.

The big man ordered his noon meal from the room clerk, and gave him a quarter to see that the tray was delivered to his room promptly. As with many fat people, he avoided eating in public. When he was alone or in the privacy of his house or room, he gorged.

Now he had three steaks, and three orders of two vegetables, two bowls of stew, six rolls, three bottles of beer, and half a cherry pie. When he finished eating he lay down on the bed for a rest.

A moment later he looked at his gold vest pocket watch. Only a little after two P.M. He had to try again. He went out the side door and to the smallest saloon in town where the beer cost only a nickel and where the down and outers openly panhandled for drinks.

He found the man he was looking for and waved him over. The man had done jobs for Laidlaw in Helena before. He was small, weasel faced, and whiskey thin. Usually he couldn't remember when he'd had his last meal. He subsisted on beer and crackers, but usually he forgot to eat the free crackers.

He was known as Skunk Johnson and took baths only when he fell dead drunk into a river. He sat down at the back table across from the ponderous bulk of Laidlaw and eyed the mug of draft beer waiting there.

"Help yourself, Skunk," Laidlaw wheezed.

The small man leaned forward in the chair, scooped up the mug and downed half of the amber fluid without taking a breath. Then he set the mug down and stared at Laidlaw.

"You want something," Skunk said. When he opened his mouth black stumps of teeth showed past thin lips. "Always want something when the beer is here first."

"Most people want something, Skunk. You want something, you want to stay drunk for a month. I can fix it for you. I can leave thirty dollars with the barkeep for you as a tab. Then you can buy a dollar's worth of beer a day for thirty days. That should keep your nose red for a month."

"Yeah, probably. But I can't do it."

"I haven't even asked."

"Know what it is just the same. You buy me another beer?"

Laidlaw waved at the barkeep who brought two more beers and set them in front of Skunk.

"I hear things," Skunk said. He finished the first beer and turned it upside down on the table. Not a drip ran out of it. "Talk gets around. There's a federal lawman in town. Your boys missed him and one got his head blown off, the other asshole's in jail."

Skunk swilled down half the second beer, and peered at Laidlaw through barely open eyes.

"You still want the lawman planted out in the graveyard, right?"

"If he had an accident I wouldn't cry over it."

They looked at each other for a minute. Skunk drained the second beer and belched. Laidlaw wiped sweat off his face with a linen handkerchief and moved back on his chair.

"You know anybody who might like to arrange an accident?"

"Can't say, off hand."

They watched each other again. Skunk snorted, shook his head.

"Shit on a platter, Mr. Laidlaw. I wouldn't touch an accident job like that for under five hundred dollars."

Laidlaw laughed. "That's two years pay for a working man, Skunk. Outrageous."

"So is losing everything you own on land down in Virginia City. Might find some help for you for five hundred." He downed the third beer without taking a breath, belched again and stood. "You get your price up where it's worth a man's life to take on the job, and I might be able to find you three good men."

"Three?"

"That's Spur McCoy, you're talking about, Laidlaw. He's known all over the West from San Francisco to St. Louis by men who claim to make a living with their guns. He's a hard man to go up against. Don't plan to fight fair if you want him to eat lead. Come to my office anytime." Skunk turned, and walked toward the bar where he slouched at his usual end spot waiting for an unwary stranger from whom he could cadge a drink.

Laidlaw finished his beer and rolled off the chair. He went out the back door. His form was easy to spot, and he had no wish to be identified yet in town. He went through the alley that led to his hotel and in the side door and to his room.

He rested on the bed for a while, then a commotion out on Main Street brought him to his window. He pushed aside the curtains and looked out. Someone was screeching down the block in front of the bank.

Even from a half a block away he knew the woman talking was Libby Adams. Why must the woman haunt him so? She was off on another tirade. This was her town. How in hell did he shut her up long enough to win his battle with the relocation committee?

Damn! With a good rifle he could almost do the job himself from here. No, the federal man would still be there. It would do no good to win the battle for the capital only to wind up at the end of a stretched hemp rope with a noose around his neck.

He had to get the lawman out of the way first. Laidlaw called the room clerk and had him send a messenger to bring Skunk to his room. He went back to the window and watched down the block. He could almost hear what the woman was saying.

In front of the bank on a quickly put together platform, Libby Adams stabbed her finger through the air at the twenty some persons listening to her. She was just getting warmed up.

"I remind all of you ladies, that we must be equal partners in the home. We are not some chattel that

can be bought and sold. We are not the property of
our husbands. We are individuals in our own right!
We are human beings. Without us there would be no
family unit. We should have an equal say in everything that goes on in the home. We can own
property. We can be accused and tried under the
law.

"And since we are subject to laws, we should be
able to voice for or against those laws and to elect
the lawmakers. Women are just as smart and
intelligent, and compassionate as men are. Men
have not given us a chance to show what we can do.
But my husband did. Alexander Adams had no male
heir, no heir at all, so he trained me to take over his
businesses.

"I've done a good job managing them and making
them grow. Ask anyone in town.

"Another thing. Women pay taxes. I pay taxes.
Do you know how much tax my companies paid to
Lewis & Clark county last year? You would be
surprised. It amounts to almost one third of the
total budget of the county!

"Yes, over thirty percent. Yet I have no say
whatsoever in how that money is to be spent. I don't
even have a vote to elect the members of the board
of county commissioners! That is simply taxation
without representation. If you remember correctly,
we fought a war with England over that one. Maybe
I'm about ready to fight a war with the county over
taxation."

She paused and looked around. There were more
men than women. She saw two members of the
county board listening intently to her. Good!

"What do you think would happen if I refused to
pay my county taxes? What if the county suddenly
had one third less money than they had last year?

Mr. Commissioner, what would you do then? What if I deny you the right to vote in the state and county elections? What would you do? Walk in my moccasins for a mile and see how it feels!"

The women in the group cheered and she let a soft smile touch her stern face.

"Gentlemen, ladies, all I'm asking for is what the women of Wyoming have. They have the vote. They had it from the very first plans to form the Wyoming Territory. All women over twenty-one in that territory vote on state and local officials and every concern on the ballot.

"You must give us the vote. We deserve it. You must start treating us like equals, not inferiors. If you don't, the day is going to come when the women will rule, and men will be treated as second class citizens!

"Look at it another way. The law says women are too dumb to vote. Fine. Then I am too dumb to vote, and I'm also not smart enough to run my businesses here in town. I made a count. I employ over four hundred people here in town. Of those four hundred, three hundred and forty-seven are heads of households.

"If I'm too dumb to run my businesses, I better just close them down. That means three hundred and forty-seven families in town will be out of work. Will the men of the county support them? Will the county poor farm take them in? Will the Board of Commissioners find food and clothing for them all?

"Makes you stop and think, doesn't it? The only conclusion has to be that women are just as smart as men. If we educate our girls as well as our boys, they will be doctors and lawyers and engineers and just as smart as their male counterparts. It's long overdue for the United States, and the Territory of

Montana to wake up, and give women the vote!"

Spur came running up. He had spent too much time with Will Walton. Damn, she was at it again. He saw a man in the crowd touch his six-gun. Spur was on him in a whisper. Grabbed the hand on the gun and powered the man six feet to the rear of the small crowd.

"What the hell?"

"Take your hand off that iron, mister!"

"Damn, what's the matter with you?"

"Looked like you were about ready to use that hogsleg."

The man shook his head. "Hell no. Happens I agree with the lady. I'm telling our representative in Virginia City to vote yes on her bill when it comes to the floor. Like the idea."

"Oh, fine. Excuse me. Just trying to protect the lady."

Man nodded. "I hear there's some cause to do just that."

Spur left the man, went to the edge of the platform and stared hard at Libby. She saw him, grinned, then waved at the crowd and stepped off the platform.

"I thought we agreed that you wouldn't make any more speeches?"

"I agreed that you said it, I never told you I would follow your suggestion."

"Let's get inside the bank," Spur said holding her elbow. She went with him.

"Spur McCoy, you should know that I'm a direct descendent of John Quincy Adams, the sixth President of the United States. No one is going to keep me quiet until they bury me."

"That's exactly how I'm afraid someone is going to shut you up. Now let's figure out how we can come to some agreement on what you will and won't do the next two days."

"I'm a descendent of the President on my mother's side, not my husband. Her name used to be Adams, too."

Spur bobbed his head at her and they went up the steps to her office.

"I didn't plan on speaking today, the mood just hit me and I went out and did it."

"Keep better control of your impulses next time until we can talk over your plans," Spur said. "You're being unfair to me, you know."

"Unfair? How?"

"If somebody kills you, I'll probably lose my job."

She looked up at him quickly, saw his crooked grin and punched him in the shoulder.

"We certainly can't let you lose your job, now, can we?" She sighed. "All right. I'll be more careful. I'll talk over with you any more speeches I want to make." She watched Spur closely. "Did you enjoy the present I sent to you last night?"

"Enjoy? What present?"

"You know what I mean, Charity."

"She was delightful. But usually my tastes run to someone a little older, more mature, experienced."

"Are you just putting in an order?"

"Just making an observation. Oh, I also prefer brunettes." He watched her and saw her look up at him quickly, a small smile faded as she turned away. He wondered what she was thinking.

"Nice try at changing the subject, but you still must be more careful. Do you think Laidlaw is in town?"

"Probably. He's more than likely planning a party for the relocation committee as soon as they hit town. It's always been his style."

"Wine, women and song?"

"At least wine, women and whiskey, plus lots of food. I've seen him operate before."

"Describe him for me. What does he look like?"

"You'll have no trouble spotting him. Rufus Laidlaw is obese, probably around three hundred pounds and about six feet tall. He is a hard man to miss. He has a fat face, tiny eyes and he's a made to order politician. He's usually within the law, but has no moral handicaps when he wants something done."

"I'll watch for him. Are you through here, ready to go home?"

"No. I have more work to do."

"When you're ready to go, I want to take you home, just in case. I think Laidlaw will try to kill you again today."

"What about yourself? Aren't you a target, too?"

"Secondary, you're the prize."

"Oh, I did hear that the surveying crew on the right of way is moving closer. They should be in town sometime tomorrow."

"Know anything about them?"

"Not much. Most of them are trained engineers who specialize in grades and routes and finding the best passes through the mountains. I've heard that some of them can be bribed to route the line a few miles this way or that. But I've also heard that some of them are so strict and professional that they would never even listen to the offer of a bribe. They are honor bound to put the road where it should go, period."

"Sounds like a good crew."

"Spur, we simply have to get the railroad to come through here. It's the best route, nobody can dispute that. I'm just afraid of the politicos, men like Laidlaw. Somehow they might come up with enough money to sway the decisions. They'll say the route should swing south with the Yellowstone River at Livingston for about twenty miles, and then cut west through the Madison Mountain range to Virginia City."

"Railroaders hate the mountains. They'll pick the easiest way through, no matter the politics."

"I hope so. If we get the railroad and the state capital relocated here, this town will be set up for a hundred years!"

Spur left then and toured the saloons. He saw no man who looked big enough to be Rufus Laidlaw. He asked in two of the saloons if the barkeep had seen him, but the two men said they were not sure who he was.

When Spur described Laidlaw they said nobody that big had been in their places all day.

The Secret Agent cruised the three blocks long Main Street and when he saw no sign of the fat man, he leaned back in a chair next to the Helena General Store and soaked up some sun.

An old timer next to him looked over with disapproval.

"New in town?" the old man asked.

"Yep."

"No wonder. These chairs is reserved for residents and customers. You either one, young feller?"

"Nope."

"Figures. And you're too big for me to pitch out of that chair so Wally can sit there, right? Probably the next thing you'll want to do is sit there and talk all afternoon."

He looked at Spur who had his eyes closed letting the sun warm him.

"Yeah, like I figured you'll probably talk my arm

off if'n I give you half a damn chance. One thing I can't stand is a body who wants to run off at the mouth all the time. Just can't bide that no way. I had me a wife for a time, and she was of that ilk. Just talk, talk, talk, all day long so a man couldn't get a word in lengthwise. You hear that blamed woman up there at the bank today?

"Now, there was a talker. Course none of us agree with her. What she needs is a man to get her pregnant and keep her barefooted and without no clothes on and in her kitchen cooking." He grinned and then snorted. "Yeah, like to see that. Libby bare assed in her kitchen." He looked at Spur again.

"Damn, you still jabbering? Be glad when Wally gets here. Least I won't have to listen to him chattering all the time. You know what I figure about this Libby woman? I got it all thought through. Now stay with me on this. I figure that . . ."

Spur tuned the old man out and let the warm Montana sun soak into his bones. There wasn't a thing he could do right now until Laidlaw or one of his men made a move. He had Libby covered, and so far they had been lucky. He hoped that their luck was not going to change. But then with luck you can never tell.

He knew he should rock the chair down on all four legs, and get up and tour the town again. Maybe he would do that in another ten minutes. Spur McCoy relaxed, and smiled. He couldn't even hear the old man beside him in the tilted back chair talking up a storm.

8

Will Walton left the eatery on Main Street, with a full belly and a lot more positive outlook than he knew he had felt for years. He flipped a twenty-dollar gold piece in the air, caught it and headed for the livery. Spur McCoy had given it to him as a loan because of old times together. Fine man that McCoy.

Will had left his fine black at the livery that morning early when he got into town, not quite sure how he would pay for the stable rent and the feed. Now he could.

He had his pistol and a box of shells, and his saddle and small sack of possibles he had left at the livery. He was set! Now what he wanted to do was ride out and find the WW ranch. He had asked at a saloon and when two people told him the same directions he believed them.

About six miles out toward the mountains, along a stringy crick and up a small valley. He paid the livery man, saddled up and rode out with confidence brimming over. This was going to be the end of a

long search for him. He as sure of it. He would find
his family, his son, today!

He had tried three states before where there had
been WW brands registered. At two of the ranches
they were obviously not the right family and they
had no idea what he was talking about. The people
were not his people and he faded away quickly. The
third one had been burned out by Indians and the
owners had left a year before.

Now he had another chance. It *just felt different*
this time. Somehow, he knew this had to be the right
place. He was going to find his family . . . his SON!

Will blinked back the sudden moisture in his eyes
and galloped out of town to the west, then reined
down and walked the mount, not wanting to burn
her out before they got to the valley. The closer he
came to the right spot, the more certain he became.

All those years of wandering, not sure who he was
for months at a time, chasing the ghosts of men
killed five years before in the war, trying hard to
remember where he should be going, all of that was
going to end . . . and soon.

He had ridden away with confidence from the
Rebel prison camp that first day after they got the
word the war was over. He had been lucky and drew
a half worn out horse from one of the Northern
companies that opened up the camp.

He had turned west and galloped for Kansas. But
somehow he never reached it. Where had he been for
those five years? What did he do to stay alive? Will
shook his head. He would not even think about that
anymore. He was going home! The words made
emotion surge up in his throat and he could hardly
breathe for a moment. His eyes misted and he wiped
at them with his hand.

Home!

He came to the rise where he could see the valley and the crooked little stream that came out of it. The valley was a mile long, half that wide, plenty of graze for three hundred head in this green!

At the far end he saw a house, log construction, with a barn to one side and what looked like two corrals. He rode then, anxious to be sure, to tie it down once and for all that he was home, that his wandering and hunting were over.

The horse stopped at the stream to drink, and he stared ahead. The log cabin was closer now, must be twenty-four feet square, maybe bigger! Lots of work involved there.

He walked the horse then, memorizing every tree, the patches of bright green along the stream. He saw where it had overflowed with spring rains, turning the low meadow into a marsh for a while but now thick with belly-deep grass. Ahead, fir and western larch stood as sentries around the cabin and peppered the far end of the valley where the hills rose.

It was perfect! A great looking little spread. He saw the cattle long before that, but hadn't wanted to concentrate on them until he was closer. Now he did and saw that they were a mixed breed, but he could recognize none of the stock he had used.

Seven years! None of the animals would be the same even if they drove some breeding stock up here, which would be doubtful.

He came out from behind a copse of brush and hardwood trees along the creek and headed down a narrow lane the last quarter mile to the house.

It even had hollyhocks growing by the corner. His wife, Martha, had always been partial to hollyhocks.

He was two hundred yards away when a young boy of six or seven came away from the well house with a hoop and stick, when the hoop fell over, the boy saw him. He stood still for a moment, then when he was sure the man rode toward the house, he ran quickly to the side door and vanished.

A woman soon stepped from the side door a shotgun in her hands. She was short, chunky with stringy yellow hair. His heart skipped a beat. So long! It had been such a long damn time! Was it her, was this woman really his wife?

He rode forward, kept his hands where they had been on the reins. He didn't want to come all this way, all five years, and then be shot down as a robber.

His horse kept walking forward. He stared at the woman's face. Too far yet. At fifty yards he wasn't sure. Then at twenty he was. A surging joy filled him. Will walked the black horse up to within ten feet of the woman.

"Hello Martha, it's been a long time." He had practiced a hundred thousand times what he would say when he found her. Now only this had come out.

She looked at him. "How come you know my name?"

"Don't you recognize me, Martha. Mite older now, been seven years. Don't you remember back in sixty-three when I left the WW ranch in Kansas and went to war . . ."

Small muscles tightened around her mouth. She looked toward the barn, then on west.

"You best get moving on. My husband don't allow no grub stake riders around when he's not here." She made no move to lift the shotgun which now pointed at the ground.

"Martha, I hear you had a baby, a boy. I never did see him. Didn't you get my letters?"

"Why would I get letters from a stranger? You

best move out of here before my husband comes."

The shotgun muzzles came up now, both pointing dead square on his chest.

"Martha, I'm going to take off my hat, slow and easy. Don't do nothing rash with that scattergun. Slow and easy take off my hat. You'll recognize me then." He slid off the battered black hat and held it over his chest. "Remember, Martha? I met you on Tuesday and the next Saturday I came courting and we got married a week later. Remember, Martha? Emmy Lou James stood up with you, and my best man was Hic Warren. Remember?"

"Best just move on, stranger."

"Martha, I've been hunting you for five years. I got wounded in the war, made me forget things, sometimes for months at a time . . ."

"My husband got killed in the war, at the Wilderness. Nobody seen him after that. Don't know what kind of stories you been hearing."

"My name is William Walton. That WW brand is still mine, legal and registered in Kansas City. You're my wife Martha, and that boy must be my son. What's so hard to believe about that, Martha?"

"My husband got war-killed. Told you. Can't stand here all day."

She put her finger on the trigger. "You aiming to move on, or do I have to dig a grave?"

"Why did you sell our place in Kansas, Martha? It was a good little spread."

"Sold the place when I was a legal widow. Judge said any soldier not coming home twelve months after the war was legal and declared him dead. Made me a widow. Got the paper somewhere. My husband was war-killed. Admit you look something like he used to. But you old now."

"So are you, Martha, but I know you."

She called the boy who came and stood beside her.

"You bring those extra shells, Will, like I told you?" she asked the lad.

He held up four more 10-gauge shotgun shells. She lifted the muzzle and blasted a load of shot six feet over Will's head.

"Martha, I got my discharge paper. I can prove I'm Will Walton."

"Don't matter none. I got my paper too. All legal and honest. I'm married again. Good man. Big German man who would break you in half. You best move on down the trail."

Quickly she broke the shotgun open pulled out the spent shell, pushed another one in and had it trained on Will before he could move.

"You always was good with weapons, Martha. You dead set on this?"

"My man got war-killed. Got a paper."

Will took one more good look at the seven year old boy. He had Will's brown hair, his lean chin and long nose.

"Reckon I better move on, then, your mind made up. You owe me for the ranch. Gonna ask a lawyer back in town about it. Legal dead ain't real dead."

She motioned with the weapon.

He turned the horse.

"Still time to change your mind, Martha. Court might figure you moved a little quick after that twelve months."

She shook her head.

"What's my son's name. You can tell me that. Looks just like me. What's your name, son?"

"Will, William Walton, Jr. Are you . . ." He looked at his mother who was grim faced staring at the man on the horse. "Are you my real Pa?"

"Shore am, Will. Mighty proud to meet you after

all this time. I got hurt in the war, forgot who I was for a long time. Not too sure where I was even. But now I'm well, I know who I am and I know who you are. I'm your real Pa. You tell your Ma that when I ride off.''

He turned and kicked the horse in the flanks. The black exploded away from the spot and three seconds later the shotgun roared, speading instant death where he had been sitting only moments before. He looked back and saw her swing the gun, but he was out of range of the pellets by then.

Tears streamed down his face. He stopped the black and turned to look at the spread again. The woman went in the cabin at once, came out and took the boy with her to the barn. A minute later he saw them both mounted, and riding to the east. He moved down trail.

She would be going to talk to her husband. Now there was nothing else for him to do. He had to go back to town and talk to Captain McCoy, then see a good lawyer. Some lawyers would not even talk to you unless you showed them money first. He would see, he would see.

Behind him Martha Walton rode toward the east range.

"Is he my real Pa? Is he Ma?"

"You just ride and forget what he said. We do have ourselves a problem. Hans will know what to do. That's why he's around. You don't worry none about your Pa. If he had wanted you or me he would have found us a long time ago. That man was just somebody your Pa talked to during the war. Still happens. Strangers bothering us war widows.''

"He did look like the picture you got, Ma."

"Hush up and help me find Hans.''

"Looked a lot like me, Ma."

"You tryin' to get a clout 'long side the head, boy?"

"No, Ma."

"Then hush up. We got troubles enough without you starting to yowl like some old hurt tom cat."

"Hans said he was going to find those strays," Will Jr. said.

"Where's that?"

"Out by the far windmill."

They found Hans twenty minutes later. She told him straight out what the man said.

"Is he who he says?" Hans asked, his broad German face stern.

"Don't matter for sure, he thinks he is."

"I want to know. It does matter."

"Reckon he probably is. Been a long time."

"Then we have a problem. You have a problem."

"We both at fault, Hans. You just as much as me. You said to do it, showed me how and all. Law will say you're to blame, too."

Hans frowned and put his hands on his hips. They all were dismounted around the stock tank beside a twenty foot tower windmill. The blades spun around, the drive arm worked up and down and with each cycle, another gush of water ran down the wooden trough and into the tank.

"There's only one way to take care of it," Hans said.

"We could move again."

"No, I told you, this was the last time we move," Hans said. "We're on a good spread. We stay put. He's the one who rides on."

"He won't, not Will. Stubborn man once he thinks he's right."

"So we're back to the one answer," Hans said.

"What's that, Ma? What you aiming to do?"

"Shut up, boy!" Hans roared. "When we want your mouth working, we'll ask you." He looked back at Martha. "You're in this feet first too, you know. You got a better way to settle it?"

"Move on. Or take him in. We could take him in and . . ."

"He's your husband. Think he'd take kindly to your living with me these past five years?"

"No, Will wouldn't understand that. I thought he was war-killed. We both did. A year after the war and he wasn't back yet. Judge agreed with me. Then when you come to the house that night, just seemed natural."

"Now Will suspects, he'll blow my head off. I got to get him before he kills me."

"Must be a better way, Hans."

"If you figure one out, you tell me. We're riding back to the house so I can get a rifle and some more shells. Then I'm heading out to do what has to be done."

None of them spoke on the way back.

At the ranch house, Will Jr. took two of the horses to the corral and unsaddled them. When he came back, Hans was ready to ride.

"You gonna shoot my Pa, Hans?"

"Shut up, kid."

"Hans, we could tell Will flat out it's all legal. I got the judge paper making him legally war-killed. We're legal anyway we want it. We could give him half the ranch somehow. Must be a better way than this."

"And when he finds out about the other?"

"No way he has to find out. I won't tell him. Will here didn't know nothing about it."

"He'd find out. There's more coming the letter

said. They'll want to check his signature for sure this time. Him being on a long cattle drive won't work again."

"I've changed my mind, Hans. I can't do this to Will. He was my husband for three years."

"I been with you for five years, that mean nothing?"

"Course." She turned and let the tears come. When she looked back she wiped the wetness away. "Hans, don't go. Stay here and let's think through all the ways to settle it. Must be a better way than this."

"Sure, for you. Turn me in and say I done it 'cause I signed the paper, and they send me to prison, you get your husband back and all the hard work I've put into this place." He swung up on the gray and shook his head. "Not a chance, woman. I've earned what I have here, and no wandering range bum is going to cheat me out of it!"

He turned and rode away.

"No, Hans, don't!"

Her plea was lost in the clatter of hooves on the hard ground of the trail toward town.

9

Will Walton paused on his black at the far end of the mile-long valley and turned, staring back at the spread where his wife and son were. Once he saw them riding across the valley toward a far finger canyon, then they were out of sight.

He couldn't simply ride away. Not after such a long search, so much pain and hurt and anguish. He had to get off the black and sit on the rich grass. He never had graze like this in Kansas.

Why wouldn't she admit who he was and take him in? He was legally dead she had said. A judge gave her a paper. She had probably married again. Reasonable.

He looked away and shouted. "No!" Why had it happened to him? Didn't he have enough problems? For a moment he recalled one or two of his days of wandering. The times came back in snatches, and none of them were pleasant. At least he could not remember ever being in jail.

He watched the clouds skittering over the mountains far to the west. The Rockies! He had often heard of them.

Why had she turned him away? It had to be more than a new husband. What? He stirred, then lay back in the grass and stared at the sky. Someday he would know. Now he had to do the logical, rational thing—go back to town and talk to McCoy, then talk to the best lawyer Helena had.

Will rode slowly. He had no great desire to bring the law against his former wife. Or was she still his wife? He knew some of the missing during the war had been declared legally dead. But what happened to him? Was he still married or not? He would let a judge decide that.

He would live with it either way. He admitted that he hardly recognized his wife. She had changed. She wasn't just plump now, she was fat, and not that pretty anymore. Ranch life was cruel to any woman, it wore her down, destroyed her youth and beauty and soon she was another work animal. It was twice that hard on a man.

He came to a long arm of timber that slanted diagonally up a ridge, down through a small feeder stream valley and upward into the foothills. He knew enough about the terrain now so he could save a mile by cutting over the ridge and through the timber.

Mostly lodgepole pines here and a few Engelmann spruce, so there was less underbrush. Someday the loggers would move in here. But not until the railroad came through so they could get the lumber out at a fair price. The days of wagon trains hauling goods out of the mountains was almost over.

The trains would revolutionize commerce in the next twenty years. It was an exciting time to be alive. So much happening. The West opening up so quickly, people on the move. New inventions coming out every year.

A half mile ahead he saw what looked like the same horse at the side of the trail. The rider was off giving his steed a blow. He wiped the horse down as Will rode up.

The man looked up and smiled. "Crazy horse tried to run away with me. Just broke her couple of weeks ago. I think she's got it out of her system now. Heading for town?"

The man was big and blond. Will said he was going that way. The man eyed him a minute.

'Wouldn't be looking for work, would you? On my way to town to pick up a good man with steers. Got some roundup and branding work to do, and I could use another hand. Just a small spread. You interested?"

Will pushed his hat back and crooked his left leg around the saddle horn. He took out makings and rolled himself a brown paper smoke.

"Could be. I been around cattle most of my life."

"Look a little thin. Sure you could put in a dawn to dark day on the range?"

"Does a horse have four feet?"

The man laughed. "Well, guess I should know your name."

"Will Walton," he said. Will saw in a haze as the man dug for his six-gun. Will's came up fast and first and a shot sang past the man's right arm so close it stopped the man's draw before he had iron out of leather.

"You know me, but I'm not sure about you. Must be Hans, who's been living with my wife for past five or six years."

"Got me all wrong, friend," Hans said, his hands well away from his weapon. "Me, I'm just a ranch hand. Woman didn't know nothing about cattle and

I did. When you didn't come home after the war, she just natural kept me on."

"Most ranch foremen don't sleep with the owner."

"Hell, after three years it just sort of happened."

"That's the way you die, it just sort of happens, today. You stole my ranch, my cattle, my wife and even my son. Why should I let you live?"

"I'm not even sure you're who you say you are. You got a paper says so? You prove it any way?"

"I can. Martha. When she's naked she's got a silver dollar size birthmark on her left thigh, high up to her crotch. That enough? She's also got two moles on her left breast. Now how could I know that less I had bedded the lady, who is my wife. You got anything else smart to say before I kill you?"

"Yeah, where the hell you been the last five years? Why didn't you come back? She waited for you a year after it was over? You didn't come 'cause you was crazy out of your head, right? I heard about men like you. Got so sick of killing that they went crazy and tried to forget it and forgot everything.

"While you were running around all crazy, I was doing your work on the ranch, branding, cutting out stock to sell, driving them to the railhead. I worked for everything I got, I didn't take it away from you, I built up the herd."

"My herd. It was still my ranch, my wife, my son."

"So go ahead and kill me. But I bet you can't. You killed too much during the war. Now you can point that thing, but you won't gun me down in cold blood. Not a chance."

"Try me and see, asshole!"

"Aim to. You still half out of your head. Crazy man."

"I was, but I saw my son. I'm fine now. No more

blackouts, no more spells when I can't see straight and don't know where I am. That's all over. First I kill you, then take over my spread again and my wife if she wants to stay. But my son stays, that's for damn sure!''

Will wondered if he was slowing down, or maybe he *couldn't shoot a man anymore.* Hans faked to the left, surged back, then went left and kicked out with his boot, spinning the six-gun from Will's hand. Hans turned and ran.

Will dropped to the ground, grabbed his gun again, but by then Hans was into the timber, past two big lodgepole pines. Will rolled to get behind some protection as a round slammed into the ground where he had been.

"I got plenty of time, Will. You're a dead man. You'll never get to town. I know every inch of this woods and the range. We're still four miles from Helena.''

Will sent a round into the brush where he thought the voice came from, but heard only a laugh.

Will saw the man running for his horse which he had whistled for. He had a shot but didn't pull the trigger. For just a flash his mind saw a Reb soldier and his horse. The smoke of the Wilderness came and the saplings and thorn brush, but Will beat the images back, smashed them down, refused to accept them.

Slowly his vision cleared and he was still in Montana. The gunman was on his horse and vanishing into the pine trees.

Will mounted and rode after Hans. He was trailing him, which meant going slower, but making sure he didn't walk into an ambush and be shot from his saddle.

He saw the angle the horseman took led uphill and

away from town. That figured. Spur tracked him for
a half hour, then came to a dense woods, that
reminded him too much of the Wilderness. A rider
could sit in there ten yards without being seen.

A simple trail double back would put a man in
perfect position for an ambush. Will rode to the left,
around the ambush spot by fifty yards, then
doubled back and waited in an ambush of his own.

Hans came out of the dark woods, fast, charging
through the lighter brush and trees, aiming for the
top of the ridge. Will waited until he was not more
than twenty yards away and fired three times with
his pistol.

He knew the first round was high, pulled it down
but by then, Hans had leaned almost out of the
saddle. Will's next round hit the saddle horn and
slanted away and his third round would have un-
seated a rider in the saddle.

Then Hans was away into the brush.

Will followed him. There was nothing else to do
now. He figured Hans had decided to make Will stay
dead with a pair of .44 slugs. That would solve his
and Martha's problem. Will wasn't enthusiastic
about the solution. He got off his mount and
checked the ground where the trail faded, came up
with it across a hard packed earth area where the
horse had gone hard through a small creek and up
the far side.

The tracking became slower. Will worked deli-
berately. Now was no time to make a mistake. It
could be his last if he did. He checked the route,
moved ahead a hundred yards and found the tracks
again, then once more leaped ahead only to lose the
prints and have to go back to the last sighting.

The trail led up the slope into heavy forest of
Douglas fir and ponderosa pine. A sudden shot

slammed into the intense silence of the woods. No round came near Spur. The man ahead could have dropped his six-gun, or shot at a snake.

Will galloped ahead quickly toward the sound of the shot. He came around a pair of three-foot thick Douglas fir trees standing almost side by side and saw the problem twenty yards ahead. It was a draw, free of brush, but heavily matted on each side.

Hans sat on his nervous horse facing the biggest Grizzly bear Will had ever seen. It had reared up on its hind legs and stared from small eyes at the man and horse. The bear stood nine feet tall and looked down on the rider.

Hans had his six-gun out but did not fire again. A wounded Grizzly is a horrendous foe, Will had heard. The bear roared and swiped at the horse which jittered backward, head twisting and turning. Hans had trouble enough just to stay seated on the animal.

He fired again into the dirt beside the Grizzly's big feet but the huge beast stood his ground.

There was no time for Hans to pull the heavy Sharps rifle from his boot. He moved the prancing horse backward, looked at both sides, but there was no way out. He had to back uphill.

Will had drawn his pistol and sighted in on Hans, then let his weapon's aim drift over toward the bear.

In a move that caught both men by surprise, the Grizzly jolted forward and with one ponderous swipe of a huge front paw, slammed the side of Hans' horse to the left, breaking its neck, tumbling Hans to the ground. He rolled as he hit, came to his feet running and wedged between a pair of trees on the edge of the ravine and scampered into the thick brush where the monster Grizzly would have trouble following.

Will's horse had heard the death cry of the other animal. It bucked unexpectedly and Will barely held his saddle. He swung the animal around and charged back up the gully. At the first opening he turned right the same direction Hans had moved.

He rode past a big ponderosa pine into a small opening in the brush when a pistol shot slapped at him. The hot lead ripped apart the air an inch from his skull and faded into the distance.

Will threw himself off the horse to the left, hit the ground hard and held onto his pistol. He was infantry, not a horse soldier. Will listened to the horse crashing through the brush for a dozen yards, then she stopped and all was quiet.

A branch broke to his right. Will lifted around a ponderosa and scanned the area. A slight movement of a young pine tree caught his attention. It stopped, then moved again. He watched the spot. A leg swung forward and Will pounded two shots into the space just above the leg. He heard a groan and something crashed to the ground.

As soon as Will fired he rolled to the left to another tree and stared around it on the opposite side as before.

Nothing.

He heard nothing, saw no movement. Slowly he began to circle the spot. He had to know for sure if Hans was hit, dead or only playing dead.

It took him fifteen minutes to worm through the woods silently, using cover wherever possible. At last he came to the spot he wanted, about ten yards from his former target and slightly above it.

There was a body there, all right. Will stared at it, torso, legs, one hand, the other arm thrown over the head. He could not see the man's face.

Dead? Will wondered. He moved closer, but there

was no reaction. He threw a rock at the body, but it did not flinch or move. Was he wasting time on a dead man?

Will lifted and slid behind a big pine. He looked out from ground level. He was six yards from the body now, still there was no way to see the face. It was covered by the one arm and some brush.

Will held the six-gun in both hands and walked forward, ready to fire at a moment's notice.

There was no notice. The hidden hand held a gun and it exploded twice in the blink of an eye. Both rounds hit Will. The first caught him high in the thigh and spun him around. Before he fell a second round slammed into his chest, on the right side, shattering a rib and puncturing his lung.

He jolted backward from the second round and lay stunned. He was in such deep shock that he couldn't move, couldn't speak. His eyes were open but for a few minutes they were frozen in place.

Hans, the "dead" body, lifted from the branches he had used to cover his face but leaving room for him to see out, hurried to Will. He held his six-gun trained on Will.

With one boot he lifted Will's right arm. It dropped like a dead weight. With his knife he drew a thin blood line down Will's cheek. Will didn't react. He couldn't, for the moment he was paralyzed.

Hans stood, aimed at Will's forehead and said, "Bang, bang," laughed softly and then turned.

"Now to find his goddamn horse before it wanders off." He frowned for a moment. "He died too easy. I wanted it to last longer." Hans shrugged and hurried to find Will's black horse.

Will lay there as if dead.

But he was still alive. He had heard everything Hans said. Now he waited for his body to die or give him back some powers. The sensations came slowly. First his eyes rolled and responded. He could move them, look at what he wanted to!

Next his sense of pain returned. His chest exploded with an agonizing pain that made him want to be paralyzed again. The agony seemed to peak, and then recede enough that he could manage it. His leg began to hurt and that's when he realized he had been shot in two places.

Hans had played possum on him, and the trick had worked. It had killed him. Will knew he was going to die. Doctors just didn't know how to patch up the kind of wound he had in his chest. His lungs were both on fire.

Slowly his legs began to work, then his arms. He rolled over and tried to sit up. It took him five minutes. He was a dead man, he knew. Will wasn't sure where he was, but it had to be a mile off the old wagon road he had followed. His only hope was to get there and pray help came past on the road.

Each time he breathed, fresh fires scorched his lungs. He tried to suck in air as gently as possible.

How could he move a mile through the brush and timber?

If only his horse were here he would have a fighting chance. His horse. He called. His voice came out a croak, but the name, "Blackie" somehow made it through. He clutched at his chest after the call. It hurt so much tears sprang to his eyes.

Four times he called the horse. The last time it was almost a shout, and he had some hope. Then he remembered that Hans' horse had been killed by the Grizzly and he had tried to find the black.

Will checked the position of the sun. Getting low. Maybe three in the afternoon. Time had flown on him again. He could sit right there and die. Or he could rip up his new shirt and make a bandage for his leg to stop that blood. No way to stop the blood starting to pool in his lung.

Five minutes later he had his leg wound wrapped and bandaged. The bleeding stopped. Good. Nothing he could do for his lung. He made one more try at calling the horse.

After the call he coughed and spit up blood, and he remembered what the Rebel soldier had said at the Wilderness about wounded men who spit up blood. Half dead already.

He heard something behind him. With a great effort, Will turned his head and saw his black mount push her head through a clump of brush. He called again, softly. The mare nickered and walked forward, stopping six feet in front of him.

Now what? He did not have the strength to get on the horse. There was no convenient stump of fallen log. The horse was not trick trained to lay down so he could roll into the saddle.

He thought it through again, then whistled and the horse came forward again, nearly stepping on his extended leg. She stopped beside him.

The stirrup! If he could reach up and grab it, and he could convince the horse to walk forward, she could drag him to the wagon road.

He reached as high as he could. The bottom of the stirrup was still three inches above his head. Will closed his eyes. He would die right here if he didn't catch that damn iron! He used one arm and pushed up, then surged upward with his right hand and grabbed for the stirrup.

A wave of pain battered through his body such as he had never felt before. He screamed, his whole system seemed to be on fire and bombarding his nervous system with agony signals.

He missed the stirrup.

Again he tried it to the same kind of pain, but this time his fingers closed around the iron and he held on. The horse unused to that kind of pressure on the saddle skittered toward him, then away. He held on.

"Whoa, girl. Whoa down!" She steadied. He tried to pull himself up to a standing position, but there was no strength left in his legs. He had lost too much blood, he decided. A wave of blackness swept toward him, but he dodged it and held onto the stirrup.

He had to get her moving. "Okay, girl, let's move. Giddap!" She took one hesitant step and stopped. "Come on, girl, Giddap!" She took another step, then a third and he felt his heels drag in the dirt as she pulled him along the ground.

How did he direct her? He didn't. He couldn't. He had to hope that she headed downhill toward the wagon road. It was the only thing he had left.

After fifty yards he swung around and let the pains sear through his chest as he reached up with his left hand and now held the stirrup with both.

The pain in his chest came in surging rushes that left him giddy and light headed. When the blast passed, he could open his eyes again. He saw now that the black had picked a downhill course through a gentle valley that had no timber and little brush.

For a moment he felt strong enough to try to stand, but after getting one leg up the other buckled and he nearly lost his grip on the stirrup. As he looked around he remembered none of the landmarks. He had never been in this valley before. The black wanted a drink, so she walked into the foot deep stream and stopped and drank.

The ice cold water on his feet and legs buoyed his spirits for a moment, then he realized his shoes had filled with water and there was nothing he could do about it.

The mare moved again, pulling him out of the water, back to the soft grass. His arms were like lead clubs. He had lost most of the feeling in them. He figured his arms would tear away from his shoulders at any minute.

Then they did.

He fell with his face in the grass as his hands came off the stirrup and it took him a moment to realize it. The relief in his arms was so wonderful he wanted it to go on and on.

"Whoa!" he called. The black stopped six strides away. If he called her back, she would turn around and drag him back the way they had come. He had to go where she was.

A few inches at a time would be the best he could do. He had to move forward. He pushed with his good leg, and pulled with his hands and elbows. Pushed and pulled, inches at a time.

It took him five minutes to cover the ten feet. Then he surged up and missed the stirrup. The pain in his chest almost knocked him out. He lay there gasping.

The second time he tried he caught the metal stirrup and got the black moving again.

Will began to count to take his mind off the pain. He closed his eyes and counted horses in a field, he counted steers as they came down a branding chute, he counted buffalo as they charged across the railroad tracks in Kansas.

"What the hell is this?" a voice boomed out at him from the darkness.

Will opened his eyes, looked up at a man towering over him. He was a farmer in overalls and a straw hat.

"God A'mighty, you're shot up bad!" He bent and pried Will's hands from the stirrup. "Easy now. Easy. Got a wagon here loaded but plenty of room for you on some loose hay for a mattress. You like a shot of whiskey? Shouldn't hurt that wound none. Gonna hurt some as I lift you into the wagon."

It didn't hurt, it spun Will into a frenzied scream that carried him into blessed unconsciousness.

The farmer grunted and lay Will on the straw, then covered him up with a blanket and got his rig moving down the road toward town. He urged the two plow horses along at a faster rate than usual. The farmer scowled as he watched the man. He'd been shot at least twice, but he was still alive. He wondered how far the horse had dragged the man. By rights he should be dead.

The farmer stopped in front of Dr. Harriman's office and ran inside. The medic came outside and shook his head. Between them they carried Will into the office and lay him on a table.

He regained consciousness when Doc Harriman poured whiskey over his leg wound.

"Oh, damn!" Will said.

Doc looked at him. "Bad way. Who are you? What happened?"

"Will Walton. Spur McCoy knows. Tell him . . . tell him . . . Martha . . . I saw my son!" Then Will drifted back into unconsciousness.

Doctor Harriman tried for five minutes more, but there was nothing else he could do. Sheriff Palmer sat in the outer office. Doc came out and shook his head.

"He's gone. Amazing he lasted as long as he did. Lung a mass of blood, probably filled full by now." He told the sheriff what Will had said, word for word.

"This Spur McCoy knows him. He might know what it's all about. Thanks Doc."

10

Rufus Laidlaw watched the farm wagon wheel into town and heard the excitement about the man who had been shot. Tough luck. He was interested in other things. He went back into the saloon he had been drinking at and stared at his glass. He should have a report from the clerks at the hotels soon. He had paid them to tell him when any of the railroad men got to town.

He finished the afternoon with the whiskey and a moment before he left one of the desk clerks came running in.

"Just registered a man who said he was a railroader. He's in the dining room now at the Montana House hotel."

Laidlaw waddled over to the hotel and the clerk pointed out the rail man. Laidlaw sent a bottle of wine to the man's table with a card bearing his name, and waited, then walked up.

"Sir my name is Laidlaw, and I'd like a word with you if that would be possible."

The man was in his late thirties, clean shaven with

a soft look about him. He stood at once.

"Mr. Laidlaw. Thanks for the wine. Please sit down. What can I do for you, sir?"

For the moment Laidlaw was surprised by the man's cow-towing ways. He sat and let the man pour him a glass of wine.

"Understand you're a railroad man?"

"Deed I am, Mr. Laidlaw. Been in the trade for over ten years now."

"Working the area around here?"

"Not hardly. No roads in this part, not yet that is. Hear two lines are coming this direction but could be ten years before the steel and ties get here."

"I heard the same thing," Laidlaw said sensing a winning hand. "Know what route they might be taking?"

"Rumors are that they will follow the Yellowstone most of the way, maybe four hundred miles across the state. Then, God only knows where they head."

"Wondered if you might have some say in that?"

"Me? No, I'm afraid not, Mr. Laidlaw."

"Aren't you on the survey team from the Northern Pacific?"

The man smiled, sipped the wine. "Not at all. I'm a railroad engineer by trade. Right now I'm going to Omaha after a visit to my kin up in Washington Territory. I hear there are some good jobs opening up for qualified engineers so . . ."

Rufus Laidlaw pushed back his chair and stood.

"Sorry I bothered you, sir," he said, turned quickly and walked away. Railroad man my foot! Laidlaw stormed as he hurried out to the desk clerk to demand his money back.

Laidlaw moved on to the smallest hotel, but the one in town he thought had the best food. He went into his room after ordering dinner sent to his room through the room clerk. He was surprised to find a woman on his bed. Then he remembered, he had ordered one from Marie's, the best whorehouse in town.

She sat up and stretched. She wore only a thin chemise and he could see her breasts pressing outward.

"You finally get here. It costs extra to wait, you know."

He snorted and went to the bed. She pulled off the chemise and she was as ordered, big breasts and small waist. She was partly redhead and mostly blonde.

"You ready or do you just want to look and jerk off?"

"Does your mouth ever stop running? Hell, I know how to fill it up with something." He unbuttoned his fly and tugged down his pants then kicked them off.

"Get on the floor between my knees," he said.

"Jesus . . . nobody told me. . . ."

"You want me to lay on top of you, bitch?"

"God no!" she thought about it a minute. "Hell, for five dollars you got a deal."

"Thought so. Money always does it."

She stood in front of him and let him play with her breasts, then knelt and began to work over his less than totally interested third leg.

"About time," he said when she slid his erection into her mouth and began bobbing back and forth. "Don't take all night, I got work to do."

She pushed him over on his back on the bed and moved higher. Then she slid over him, plunged his hardness into her waiting vagina and pretended he was a small pony and she was the rider.

"Damn, you are a real whore, aren't you? Bet you

could make a worn out hound dog get a hardon. Oh damn!" He thrust into her hard once bellowed in satisfaction and pushed her away and reached for his pants.

"That's it?" she asked surprised.

"Hell, I ain't sixteen anymore. I don't cum for a week and a half without stopping on an all night fuck."

"Yeah, but you ain't seventy either. Had me an old codger who was sixty-five and was he a good fucker!"

"Did he pay you five dollars?"

"Nope."

"Then get dressed and get out of here before my dinner arrives. I don't let anything spoil my eating not even a sweet little pussy like you. Now move your ass."

"Yeah, that's plain to see you like to eat." She jumped back when he swung at her, then finished dressing. She grabbed his pants and took out a bulging wallet, extracted a five dollar greenback and two ones, and threw his pants back at him.

"The two dollars is a tip, you got any complaints about the service?"

"No, now get out!"

Five minutes later the room clerk let the dining room steward bring in the dinner cart. Tonight Laidlaw had ordered three complete dinners: a two pound steak, medium rare, a large plate of spaghetti, and another dinner of fresh caught fish. Each came with vegetables, salad and soup. He ate everything in sight even the half dozen rolls in the covered basket.

As he ate, Laidlaw formulated his plans. He could always think better when his stomach was filling. He had to concentrate on Spur. Once the federal officer was taken out, he would have more luck eliminating the woman. Both had to be done tonight.

The first job was to set up a small vacation for the lady. Nothing fancy, just something away from Helena for two days. That shouldn't be hard.

When he finished eating he sent for Skunk Johnson at the saloon. Ten minutes later Skunk was in his room. He told the man exactly what he wanted done, and how much he would pay. Skunk could find his own men.

"No trouble. I've got the men to do it. She'll be home tonight. I'd suggest just after dark. Now, you said two jobs."

"I have five hundred for you for those three good men we talked about before. But there has to be a guarantee. If Spur McCoy is still living my midnight, you get ten dollars a man, period."

Skunk looked at him, tipped the beer Laidlaw had provided, then nodded. "Done. You don't know nothing about it. I'll need the thirty now, to sweeten the pot a little."

Laidlaw gave Skunk three ten dollar greenbacks and the derelict walking like a man slipped out of Laidlaw's room and then out the side door. He had walked the back streets and alleys all of his life.

Spur McCoy had just finished eating dinner with Libby in the mansion, when a messenger brought him an envelope. He tried to see who delivered it, but the person was gone quickly.

Spur opened it and read it, then showed it to Libby.

"McCoy. I know you want to find out who shot Libby Adams. I can tell you who it was, but if anybody knows I told you, I'm a dead cowboy. Meet me in back of the livery stable corral tonight at eight-thirty."

Spur checked the Seth Thomas on the dining room mantle. It was a little before seven.

"You won't go," Libby said. "It's a trap, a set up to get you alone in the dark."

"Not many bushwhackers will take on a federal agent. They know three more will show up to find out what happened to the first one. It could be a lead. I'll be careful. Getting there early is part of that. I'm gone."

He grabbed his gunbelt, put an extra box of rounds in his brown vest pocket, and checked the Remington .44 New Model army revolver and shoved it into the holster. On the way out he picked up the Henry Repeating Rifle he lived with these days. it was a .44 caliber rim fire ammo model, with a 24-inch octagonal barrel with six rifling grooves inside. It weighed over nine pounds. He liked the long tubular magazine that slid in under the barrel and held twelve cartridges.

The Henry worked with a trigger guard lever. This was the weapon the Rebels said the Yanks loaded up on Sunday and fired all week.

"I don't want you to go," Libby said moving up to him. She reached in and kissed his cheek. "I was hoping we might be able to talk tonight and have a cozy fire, get better acquainted."

"Soon," Spur said. "I had something of the same ideas, maybe with a bottle of wine and some cheese thrown in. Later. I've got to check this out. I'll be careful."

He ran out the back door and the house and over two blocks before he stopped. There would be at least three of them, he figured, and it would be a kill try. But a lot of men had tried to ambush him before. He went straight out of town three blocks into the countryside, then swung around behind the livery stables. He could see the two lanterns inside where men were cleaning stalls. There was little cover behind either corral. He chose the one with the best cover, a smattering of brush about twenty yards away.

Spur settled in the back of the brush and began his watch. Just before eight o'clock he heard a horse coming. It was cloudy and dark now. Whoever it was had not taped down his saddle rattles. He had never been in battle with a horse.

Spur picked him up out of the gloom. As the horse bored into the brush, Spur moved parallel to it, barely ten feet away. The rider was not looking for any surprises. He rode to the middle of the fifty foot wide patch of brush and dismounted. He tied the horse to a tree and moved to lift a rifle from the boot.

Spur clubbed him with the side of the Remington pistol and he went down without a sound. Before he came back to consciousness Spur had stripped him of two knives, a hideout gun and a pair of revolvers.

He appeared to be about thirty. Should know better. Spur waited for him to come back to consciousness. When he did Spur could see in the moonlight that his eyes were wild.

"What the hell . . .?"

"Sloppy work," Spur said. "If I was going to try to bushwhack somebody, I'd get there an hour early, hide well, and wait. Not come jangling in on a horse ten minutes before time."

"What you talking about?"

Spur hit him in the jaw with his fist knocking him down. He sat up holding his jaw and Spur hit him again.

"Who hired you?" Spur snarled. "You've got a minute to tell me, then your own knife is going to start slicing up your hide."

"Nobody hired me. Just out for a ride."

"That's why you were pulling out a rifle?" Spur hit him again sprawling him from his sitting position into the dirt.

He sat up slower. "No more! Okay, I was waiting. I was just support for the main two up closer to the fence."

Spur had learned the information he needed. He whacked the man with the Remington pistol again, knocking him out. Then he tied his hands behind him. Tied his feet and put a gag in his mouth.

Spur moved like a moon shadow across the open space to the edge of the corral fence. It was still fifteen minutes to the deadline. He found the best hiding spot on the left side. A feedbox had been placed just outside the fence. Ten yards way were a dozen bales of straw. He slid between an alley in the bales and stood the rifle beside him. By crouching just a little he was totally hidden.

Five minutes later he heard someone coming. A man hurried to the feed box and went over the fence hiding behind it just inside the enclosure. The dozen horses moved a little but most had settled down for the night, sleeping where they stood.

At eight thirty, Spur assumed the other man was in place. He lifted up and cupped his hands pointing his voice back toward the stables.

"Hey, McCoy here." he said speaking loud but not shouting. "Who the hell am I meeting?"

The man behind the feed box spoke.

"Over this way. I got to be sure you're alone."

"I'm alone. Where are you?"

Spur saw him lift then behind the box. Spur

tipped a bale of hay off the end of the stack so it bounced near the fence.

The man behind the box powered off three rounds from his pistol. Spur had the Remington up and snapped off two rounds aiming just over the gun flashes.

A scream rattled the boards of the corral as the man behind the box slammed backwards, his weapon firing twice more into the air before he hit the ground.

Spur moved from his firing position to the end of the hay. He stared across the corral but could detect no third man. He had to be there. Then he saw a shadow gliding across the field behind the corral. The first man was the set up for the real professional gunman moving now. Sacrifice a man to get your target positioned. This guy played dirty.

The man stopped and knelt, waited, then moved again, quickly but carefully, like an army scout moving through enemy territory. Spur watched the man come near the far end of the stacks of hay. The Secret Service Agent had his Remington up and ready. When the shadow became a man, Spur thumbed back the hammer on the weapon.

The third ambusher stopped, holding frozen in place.

"One more step and you're dead!" Spur snarled.

The man tried. He jerked up his weapon, firing as it came. The first round went into the ground near his foot, the second in the ground five feet in front of him.

Spur's first round tore through the bushwhacker's chest, ripped apart his heart and drove him backwards so the spasming of his dying fingers on his gun hand sent three more rounds into the dark sky.

Spur moved up and checked him. He was dead.

A lantern came out the back door of the livery. A man held it high.

"What's going on back here?" he yelled.

"Dead men," Spur called. "Send someone for the sheriff."

Ten minutes later the sheriff had identified both men. One was a part time rancher, the other a drifter who had been in town for a month.

"The third one in the brush can talk," Spur said. He might also tell you who hired him."

"Hope so," Sheriff Palmer said. "Both these Jaspers have a new ten dollar bill in their pockets. Not a hell of a lot to get paid to try to kill a man."

"Especially not if it works the other way," Spur said. He left the sheriff to question the witness and hurried back to the mansion. He didn't like leaving Libby alone for this long at night.

Unseen at the edge of the crowd, Rufus Laidlaw scowled as he heard the news and moved away. Damnit! What now? He had taken three good tries at killing this man. Evidently he was going to have to do it himself. But not tonight, perhaps tomorrow. He would see how the rest of his plan worked out.

There might be no need after tomorrow, if the plans all worked to perfection. He continued down a side street to his hotel and slipped in the side door. There was a note in his box behind the desk man.

"Edward Scott arrived late today. He's a surveyor with the Northern Pacific. He's in Room 14."

Laidlaw continued to his room for a bottle of whiskey and two glasses, then knocked on the door to Room 14.

The panel opened and a sun burned face stared out.

"Yeah? So?"

"Mr. Scott?"

"So?"

"I understand you're with the Northern Pacific railroad."

"True."

"Do you have a minute to talk? I and my friend would like to have a small discussion with you."

"Don't see no friend."

Laidlaw held up the bottle of whiskey, and the grim faced man in Room 14 turned into a wide grin and he swung open the door.

"Always have time for an old friend, come in, come in!"

They sat on the edge of the bed and toasted each other with the good whiskey. After the fourth toast, Laidlaw got down to business.

"How is your progress on finding the route for the new railroad?"

"Fair. The Yellowstone is a godsend. Wish she extended all the way to the Snake River."

"Mr. Scott, I know the route of a railroad is usually a closely guarded secret, but these are exploratory routes as I understand, and there are three being run."

"Four, and most everybody knows where they are going."

"But the Yellowstone is the best, cheapest to build and probably will be the one chosen," Laidlsaw said.

"Hail, you said it, I didn't."

"But it is true, isn't it?"

"Probably. If you was a betting man."

"My problem is just where you'll leave the Yellowstone. I'm hoping you'll cut south with the river for about thirty miles and then drive through the mountains to Virginia City, the capital of the Montana Territory."

"Can't say, can't say. I've got a suggested route . . ." He stopped and drained his whiskey.

"You were saying there was a suggested route?"

"Yep. Just a suggestion. Figure to keep on west past Livingston to Bozeman, then swing between mountains northwest more to a camp I call Three Forks. There I'd like to charge due north and a little west to bring us right here to Helena. From there we head west and then northwest."

"I'm still hoping for Virginia City."

"Why, you got property there?"

"Sir, I am not pleased with that remark."

"Though, it's probably true. But I never insult a man when I'm drinking his whiskey so I ask your pardon."

"That's all right. I understand. I've heard that in some cases officials of the line have changed routes to run through favored towns and areas."

"True. But don't blame me for what the bosses do. I'm just a route finder, a pathfinder."

"Say you were to recommend a path through Virginia City. What would you say to a gift finding itself your way?"

"You mean take money to make a different suggestion for the right of way?"

"Couldn't hurt. Nobody would know except you and me."

"What kind of a gift are we talking about?"

"We start with a young lady I'd like you to meet for the night. She is delightful, unspoiled, clean as my sister. Then there's an envelope in my safe with five thousand dollars in it. Both those gifts are yours for that Virginia City route recommendation."

Scott picked up his glass and finished the whiskey. Then he set it down and stood. Laidlaw puffed as he stood and smiled at the raw railroader.

Laidlaw never saw it coming. The smashing right fist caught him in the eye and drove his three hundred pounds of flesh a foot backwards, ruining his precarious balance and dumping him on the hotel room floor beside the bed.

"Mr. Laidlaw, I drank your whiskey and I listened to your ideas. Don't like them. Don't like being offered a bribe to corrupt my morals and my professional integrity. Ain't nice to offer men more money as a bribe than they make in five years. Just ain't proper." He helped Laidlaw to stand.

"Hope there ain't no hard feelings. I'm a working man. Struggle to do a good job. Fact is I'm one of the best grade engineers in the country. A damn insult to offer me five thousand dollars to compromise my professional standards."

Laidlaw felt of his eyes, shook his head. He wanted to bolt for the door but the railroader was between him and that freedom.

"You should learn, Laidlaw, that if you want to bribe a railroad man you should make it worth his while. Now I ain't saying some men won't take five thousand, but not me. My reputation is worth a lot more than that."

Laidlaw felt he had heard some glimmer of hope.

"What would you consider a reasonable amount, Mr. Scott?"

"A million dollars, hard cash. That's what my reputation is worth. No idiot is going to recommend going through the heart of the Rocky Mountains just to get to Virginia City. But for a million it would be worth considering."

"Sorry, I don't have that kind of money."

"Damn shame," Scott said. This time Scott hit him on the jaw and Laidlaw went down again. It took most of the china pitcher of water from the washstand to bring Laidlaw back to consciousness. Then Scott helped him out the door, but kept the rest of the bottle of whiskey.

Rufus Laidlaw staggered back to his room and fell on his bed. His jaw ached. He was wet from the top of his head to his waist. He was supposed to check with one man about the other part of his night's mission, but he couldn't now. He rolled over on his back and bellowed in fury. He prayed that by tomorrow he did not have a large black eye. It would not be easy testifying at the Relocation Committee hearing if he had a shiner. He bathed the eye in cold water for a half hour, hoping it would keep the blood from settling in the flesh. At last he went to bed. He made a new rule for his business ethic: Never try to bribe a railroad grade engineer for less than a million dollars.

11

Sheriff Palmer told Spur about Will Walton just before he left the corral. Spur had been saddened, but not surprised. When a man comes home after seven years, he's got to expect a few changes have been made. At least Will found his family. For some reason the woman must have turned on him. There must have been a man around to help her. From what Will said just before he died, he must have seen his son, and Martha. That was good.

Spur would ride out there first thing in the morning and check with the family, try to find out what happened. He had almost nothing to go on, but in his gut he knew that Martha or some man she knew had shot Walton. That angered Spur. He would tend to it and see that the killer paid. He owed that much to Lt. Walton.

Spur hurried now as he went back along the street to the big house at the end of the block. The Adams mansion, the people called it, and it was. He bounded up the front steps and let himself in.

Charity was usually near the door. He didn't see

her. The house was strangely quiet.

"Damnit no!" Spur thundered as he ran through the house. He found Charity in an upstairs closet. Her blouse had been ripped off and her breasts showed. She was tied and gagged. Spur untied her, found her blouse on the floor and she began to cry.

It took him three or four minutes to get her calmed down. Then the story gushed out.

"They came just after dinner, four or five of them. They just opened the front door and ran inside. One of them grabbed me and two ran into the living room and found Mrs. Adams."

"Five men. Did they wear masks?"

"Yes. They were rough talking. Clothes like they were working men, miners or cowboys. One man took me upstairs and told me to undress, but I clawed his face and he slapped me and pushed me on the bed and then ripped off my blouse.

"Somebody called from below, telling the man to tie me up and push me in a closet. He wanted to do me, but he didn't have time. So he put me in the closet and I heard him leave. Then I tried to get out, but I couldn't."

Spur put his arm around her and let her cry again. Then he took her downstairs, found a bottle of brandy and told her to have a drink, to lock the doors and not to let anyone in until he or the sheriff came.

"You going after them?"

"I'm going to try. First I'm going to talk to the sheriff again."

Five minutes later Spur had told Sheriff Palmer the story. He shook his head.

"No telling where they might be. Could be here in town, but I doubt it. More likely they could be in any one of a dozen abandoned mines and mine shacks around here."

"Does the name Laidlaw, Rufus Laidlaw, mean anything to you, Sheriff?"

"I been around here for a long time. Known a lot of men. Laidlaw. He the same one who's got some Territorial office?"

"Libby says he's some kind of officer for the Territory."

"Could be Rufus Laidlaw is the same one who had the old Laidlaw mine about three miles out of town. That was one of our famous flash in the pan mines. Produced great for about fifty yards, then the vein took a right angle into another claim. Laidlaw wound up losing everything he had in the deal."

"If he's behind this kidnapping, could his men have taken Libby out there?"

"Couple of buildings still standing, but sure as hell don't sound like a smart move to me."

"That could be it. He'd figure it was such an obvious place to look I'd never think about it, or know about it."

"Possible. Can't really track them until morning, anyway."

"Draw me a map how to get out there, and I'll need some kind of flares in case I have to go into the mine."

"Got some you can have. You want me to send a few men along with you?"

"No thanks, but I would appreciate it if you could get a search started here in town, and some of the close in abandoned mine buildings."

Ten minutes later Spur had memorized the map the sheriff drew for him and was riding. He had the Henry repeating rifle and his pistol, plus extra rounds for both. Five to one, the odds sounded about right.

It took him two hours to find the right lane leading off the main stage road. He took the wrong branch and wound up at a working gold mine. After backtracking he came to the old Laidlaw dig and at once knew it was no longer abandoned. Out in the clear air he could smell a smoke for a mile, and now the smoke came clear and strong from one of two buildings ahead.

Spur left his horse by the lane and circled around the lane that led in. He spotted a lookout in a tree a quarter of a mile from the buildings. He slid past the man and left him in place.

Soon he could see a dim light in the smaller of the two structures. Working without a sound, Spur crept up to the building until he was twenty yards away in some brush. Nobody came in or out for ten minutes. He could see smoke coming out of the chimney.

He checked the area again. There were no exterior guards that he could see. He slipped from shadow to shadow, then walked across the last ten yards to the side window. It was so dirty he could barely see through. At last he rubbed some of the outside dirt off and he could see inside.

Before he recognized anyone, a gun muzzle jammed into his back. Spur spun automatically, knocked the gun away from the surprised man, kicked him in the side the way a Japanese had once taught him, and then slammed his fist into the man's unprotected jaw, dropping him to the ground unconscious.

Spur tied up the man, gagged him and rolled him under the downhill side of the cabin. He found the gun and stuffed it in his belt, then looked in the window again.

Libby was the first thing he saw. She sat, cool and

at ease at a small table playing cards with three
men. A box of kichen matches sat on the table.
Libby had the biggest stack of matches in front of
her. She was also talking up a storm, but he couldn't
make out what she was saying to the men.

Spur crept around to the front door, tested it, then
turned the handle and kicked it open. He charged
into the room with a pistol in each hand.

"Don't move, or you're dead men!" Spur
thundered. One man dove for his gun. Spur put a
slug through his chest and he flopped over dead or
dying.

One man grabbed Libby and used her as a shield.

"You shoot me, you shoot the lady first," he said
and began backing toward the other door. As Spur
turned to watch Libby, another man reached for the
iron on his hip.

Spur's round slashed through his shoulder and he
got off a shot that went wide. Spur's second round
created a neat round hole in the man's forehead
going in, but splattered blood and brains over the
far wall as it came out the top of his head.

The man with Libby drew his six-gun and Spur
dove for the floor and tipped over the table as a
shield. Two slugs thudded into it, then the door
slammed and the man was gone.

Two men dead, one tied up, one out the back door
and one in the tree. Spur jumped up and raced after
the man with Libby. The odds were getting better.
Spur saw him tugging Libby with him in the moonlight, but he couldn't fire.

The kidnapper pushed Libby in the mine tunnel
and Spur ran up to it. From what the sheriff said the
tunnel was short and there were no shafts down to
other levels. How did the man intend to hide for long
in there?

Spur found some torches at the front of the abandoned tunnel and lit one, then held it to the side of his body and began moving into the hole. He stopped frequently to listen, but heard nothing.

The mine tunnel extended thirty yards into the hill. He checked out occasional "drifts", lateral tunnels off the main one. But most were only a few yards long.

The man and Libby were still somewhere ahead.

He worked to the end of the tunnel where he found steel stakes driven into the ground. A hand painted sign said: *No trespassing. From here forward is the Jefferson Mine. Do Not Enter.*

Spur read it again, and remembered what the sheriff said about the vein of gold running directly off the claim. The metal bars had been pushed aside and Spur squeezed through. Ahead was more mine, only this one had been worked extensively. There were large "rooms" were pockets of ore had been dug out giving the tunnel a ceiling sometimes twenty feet high.

Every dozen feet there was another drift Spur had to clear. Twenty yards into the new mine he came to a shaft dug directly in the middle of the tunnel with walking space around the sides. This one still contained a block and tackle and pulleys to lift up buckets of ore from somewhere below.

Spur checked the rope and the bucket and saw that a layer of dust covered it all. The bucket had not been used for months, maybe years. Libby had not been taken down that shaft.

He moved ahead, saw something move on the tunnel almost at his feet and jumped back as a four foot rattlesnake slithered away into the darkness. He was sure the reptile had been blinded by the sudden light of the flaming torch. There could be more. He heard that snakes loved old mines.

Spur checked two more drifts, then another shaft that fell away to darkness below. This one had a wooden ladder fastened to the wall. It looked sturdy. He checked the rungs and found the center of each clean of dust. The ends were dust covered.

Someone had descended the ladder recently, maybe within the hour. He touched a piece of paper to his torch and dropped it down the shaft. It fell only ten feet to the bottom.

Spur had to investigate. He went down the ladder with one hand, holding the torch with the other. At the bottom he found footprints, including some that could only belong to Libby.

He listened. Far off he thought he heard voices. But they faded out. There was only one direction to go. He had to duck now as the new tunnel was barely five feet tall. It had no rail tracks down it as many mines did. They worked simply here with wheeled carts men pushed.

A minute of walking down the tunnel revealed only two short drifts and no more shafts. Then the tunnel forked, moving out at forty-five degree angles. He checked both for footprints, but the soil was hard and packed and showed nothing. He picked the right hand tunnel and moved faster now.

Fifty feet down it he paused to listen, but could hear nothing. Ten minutes later he came to the end of the tunnel. Picks and pry bars and drive drills lay at the head of the tunnel as if they had been dropped at the end of a working day, but never picked up again.

Spur jogged back the way he had come to the fork in the tunnel, took the other one and moved cautiously. Here and there he saw footprints. Twice he stopped to listen, and the second time he heard a woman's voice, high and irritated.

Libby!

He moved quicker. His torch burned lower. It would go out in another few minutes.

He smelled smoke. It drifted toward him now as an air shaft somewhere sucked it from the tunnel. Wood smoke. They had built a fire ahead. Spur rounded a gradual curve in the tunnel and saw the glow of a fire. He put out his torch at once and moved slowly forward, careful not to make a sound.

The voices came clearer then. The man arguing, the woman firm and positive. He worked closer until he could hear what they were saying.

"Absolutely no way anybody is going to find us in here," a heavy man's voice said. "For sure not one man, that Spur McCoy you talk about. He's no miner. He'd get lost after the first shaft. Probably down on the sixth level now blundering down one tunnel after another."

"You can't keep me here forever," Libby said her voice strong and assured. "All the food is back in the cabin. What do you have for breakfast?"

"Worry about that in the morning. Got my Waterbury, know exactly what time it is." He paused.

Spur worked silently forward. The firelight was in their eyes. Neither one of them could see beyond its glow. He had the advantage.

"I could just rip your clothes off and force you, you know," the man said.

"You might. I'm stronger than I look, and Alexander showed me ten ways to stop a man from raping me. Want to learn all ten of them?"

"Come on, you've had a man or two since Alex died. I've heard stories."

"Stories are what they are. In any event, I'd choose my lover, not the other way around."

Spur was in range. He lifted the Remington pistol. The man moved closer to Libby. She pushed him away. He laughed. Spur aimed again and just as he fired, the man lunged forward. The round aimed at his chest, caught him high in the right arm as he moved.

He screeched in pain.

The sound of the pistol shot in the tunnel was like an echo chamber slamming the sound waves around and around, bouncing them forward and back and forward again so it felt like the sound would never fade out.

The man had been flung to the side by the shot and Libby scrambled toward the sound of the gun. Spur snapped another shot at the man, forcing him backward out of the firelight.

"Come this way away from the fire so he can't see you, Libby," Spur called. She darted in his direction at once. The other man did not fire. Then Spur saw his revolver on the ground near the fire. He had been cleaning it.

"Give it up," Spur called. "Come out now and you'll only face kidnapping charges. This is a lousy place to die."

"Die? There's a dozen ways out of this tunnel," the man shouted.

"I'm betting you're wrong. The other tunnel ended. Figure this one does too. You don't know every turn in this mine."

"Know enough. I'm gone. Next time I see you I'll be topside with my rifle waiting for you to come out the entrance to the mine. Then you'll be quick dead." The man laughed and the sound trailed off fainter as he ran down the tunnel.

He had no light. Spur moved up where Libby was and she rushed into his arms.

"Oh, Spur! I'm so glad you came! It was just terrible. Can we get out of here? I hate the mines."

A scream echoed through the tunnel before Spur

could reply. He took her hand and walked to the fire, picked up two torches and lit them, then they moved down the tunnel toward another scream.

"Easy, he must be in trouble. We don't want to fall into the same trap."

They worked forward slowly. Soon they saw the edge of a new shaft that had been started. Spur pushed the torch over the edge and looked down.

A man stood on his tip toes at the bottom of the ten foot deep shaft. Shovels and buckets and picks had been stacked neatly to one side. The man was trying to reach the buckets to stand on them. The whole bottom of the pit seemed to be moving. Spur dropped one of the torches into the hole. The moving floor was a sea of rattlesnakes, shaken out of their hibernation by the human thing dropping in on them.

"For Christ's sakes, get me out of here!" the man wailed. Then he screamed as a snake blinded by the bright light struck out but missed his leg.

"No rope," Spur said. "Stand on the buckets, maybe I can reach you."

The man grabbed the torch from the floor and cleared a path through the writhing snakes to the buckets, and tried to stand on them. They caved in, rusted through. He fell and only the torch kept him from being attacked by the furious rattlers. He burned two of them and they slithered back.

Spur pulled off the light leather jacket he wore and took a firm grip on one sleeve. The other sleeve he lowered into the pit and then stretched out flat on his stomach at the edge of the hole.

"Grab it and use me as an anchor and climb out," Spur said.

The man tried to catch the leather sleeve, but missed it. Spur stretched lower and the kidnapper caught the sleeve.

"Drop the torch and grab the sleeve with both hands," Spur ordered. "Libby, sit on my back, give me some support." She lowered on him to anchor him in place.

The man in the pit grabbed the leather and put his feet on the wall. An underground seepage made the wall slippery. He tried to step up but slid down.

The torch sputtered on the floor, frying a rattler, the light coming weaker and weaker. His foot slipped again and as it dropped down, a coiled rattler struck two feet through the air and fastened its fangs on the unprotected calf. The man screamed and dropped the jacket sleeve, falling to the bottom of the pit.

Spur held the second torch low, rattlers swarmed over the man. He screamed again and again, then looked up and one large rattler struck and fastened his fangs into the kidnapper's throat. As the poison gushed directly into the human bloodstream, Spur could see death come. It was a terrible way to die. He pushed Libby off his back and stood.

Slowly he slid into the jacket and led her back toward the fire.

"He's gone?" Libby asked.

"Yes. Nobody deserves to die that way. He paid for all of his sins in full that last five minutes."

"You gave him a choice."

At the fire they paused.

"Libby, are you strong enough to climb back out of here?" he asked.

"Yes, but is it a good idea?"

"Only one left up there who can be waiting for us, no two I guess. I tied up one of them." Spur watched her. "Might be better to wait for daylight. Then the other two will probably high tail it for town and then into Idaho somewhere."

"Let's stay right here," Libby said. "He found a blanket. It's not clean, but better than the tunnel floor.''

Spur watched her, a small grin grew on her pretty face.

"We may have to sit close together to stay warm," Spur said.

"I'm counting on that. I've never stayed overnight in a gold mine before."

"Deal," he said. He found some of the square set timbers that had been broken apart in some ore car crash, and brought them back for wood. After building up the fire, he spread out the blanket and pointed their toes at the fire. He had stacked the twelve by twelve timbers on the opposite side of the fire so the heat would reflect off the timbers and toward them.

"You've made a campfire or two in your time, I'd guess," Libby said.

"A few." She sat down beside him, pushed in so their hips touched and then turned. She smiled but through it he saw the fear that was still ebbing from her features.

"They had you scared, didn't they?"

"Yes. I've never felt so alone, or so vulnerable in my life. He . . . the man back there, would have had his way with me eventually. I had figured on that. I could live through it without any worry. But I was really afraid he would never let me leave the mine."

"Your worries are over."

"All over. I'm glad you came." She reached over and kissed him, and he felt her begin to relax.

"We could just stay warm," he said.

"We could. But right now I'm so glad to be alive that I want to see how it feels to be a woman again. I don't fuck around very often."

She grinned at his surprise that she used the word. "And I don't talk dirty unless I'm really starting to feel horny. Would you please hurry up and give me a little bit of encouragement?"

12

Spur watched Libby and slowly grinned. "Seems like I could at least offer more than encouragement." He bent and kissed her lips and she smiled at him.

"You can do better than that," she said.

Libby's mouth was open when he kissed her the next time and he let his tongue dart into her hot, eager opening. She caught his tongue with her teeth and growled at him, then let go and tried to get her tongue into his mouth.

For a moment they battled, then he let her enter and as she did his hand slid between them and closed around one of her covered breasts.

"Oh, god yes!" she said, then pushed back inside his mouth and pressed against his hand. Her mouth came away from his and nibbled at his ear, then she nestled against him.

"Tell me how you like to make love the best," Spur said, his hand working on the buttons of the dress top.

"With a man," she said impishly. "Although it's

interesting with a woman. I've never had a more tender loving than with another female. Another woman seems to know exactly what pleases a female."

She kissed him and rubbed his crotch where she felt the growing erection.

"Of course a woman's fingers are no real substitute for the real thing!" She worked at unbuttoning his pants. Spur spread the top of her dress open and lifted the soft silk chemise. Her big breasts swung out full and bouncing as they glowed in the soft firelight.

"God but breasts are beautiful, do you realize that? Most animals use the rear end to attract the male. But with women the breasts have been developed down through the ages to attract the male of the species and also to suckle her child. So first great tits are essentially for beauty but practical, too."

"Now you're getting poetic. I've never heard of a man who didn't go wild over bare tits."

He kissed her and slowly pushed her down on the blanket. She finished the kiss, then sat up.

"I want to undress you first. Every stitch. Right now." She patted his bulge. "Darling, you'll have to wait your turn, I like all parts of a man."

She took off his jacket, then his leather vest and his shirt.

"Oh, a hairy chest! I do love to play with man tits through his chest hair." She bent and kissed them both, then moved her kisses down his hard belly to his big heavy brass belt buckle.

"Oops . . . some more undressing to do here." She opened his belt and the last of the fly buttons and pushed his pants down. Spur wore cut off drawers and she jerked at them, eager to get to the important parts as she had said.

"My stars! Look at him! Such a big one. She laughed. "He's a big boy, but I bet he can do a man's job."

She pulled his boots off, then his pants and drawers and warmed her hands over the fire. Then she turned and began a strip tease for him, slipping out of her chemise first, letting her dress top fall to her waist.

For a few moments she did a sexy little dance, waving her breasts at him, humping her hips toward him and then going to her knees in front of Spur and letting one breast dangle so he could kiss it and chew on it.

"I didn't realize I was so hungry," Spur said munching away.

"Just leave some room for dessert," she said. She pulled away and lifted the dress off over her head. Instead of the usual knee length drawers common for women of the day, she wore silk panty underwear that fit loose and inviting.

"Like my short panties?" she asked. "All the women in Paris are wearing them I hear."

She knelt in front of him, her big breasts bouncing, the soft pink areolas large and glowing with hot blood. Her nipples stood up tall, enlarged by her desire.

"I'd rather see you not wearing them," Spur growled, his hands reaching for her.

"Tear them off me with your teeth! Bite your way right through to the soft, wet, and wonderful place!"

Spur bent forward, pushed her back on the blanket, her legs spread and he lowered his face into her crotch. She moaned in delight. He caught the silk fabric in his teeth and jerked upward. The fabric tore. He held the side of the panties with his hand and bit and ripped upward, exposing a slice of white thigh. Again and again he bit and tore at the silk with his teeth until it hung in shreds over her crotch. Then he parted the strands and moved toward her black muff. He parted the rich midnight hairs and exposed her pulsating quim.

The outer lips were swollen already speading outward. He bent and kissed her pussy softly, then again and she trembled.

"Do that once more and I'll squirt all over you!" she yelped. He kissed her again and she screeched in pleasure, her body jolting and pounding upward, her hips doing a little dance as he watched. Again and again tremors pulsated through her body, shaking her, rattling her until she growled in animal delight. She pulled his naked body on top of hers and her hips pounded upward a dozen times as the spasms kept rocketing through her slender body.

"My god! Nobody has ever done that for me before!" She kissed him and then licked her lips. "I can at least do the same for you." She gathered their clothes to make a pillow for her head lifting it forward so she could accept him, then motioned to him. Spur straddled her shoulders with his knees and bent forward.

Her hand caught his penis and pulled it down into her mouth. She took a deep breath and nodded and he began to slide in and out of her.

Spur had been so worked up it didn't take long. She held off on it as long as he could, then she moaned in anticipation and he couldn't stop it, and the life substance of the universe jolted through him and gagged her momentarily until she swallowed. Then she sucked him dry and at last he rolled away and panted on the blanket, as she lay on him like a warm cover.

When Spur could talk he bobbed his head. "Marvelous, wonderful. Who taught you that?"

"Alex, he taught me everything I know. God bless you Alex, even though you have ceased to exist."

He looked at her. "Alex is not in heaven?"

She laughed. "Long ago Alexander convinced me of the total folly of all religion. He said religion is for fools, the lazy, or those who need some crutch because they are too weak to stand on their own two feet and face life. They want somebody to blame and commiserate with."

"But religions have been around since man crawled out of the slime of the prehistoric oceans millions of years ago."

"So has strong drink, evil men and prostitutes, but nobody says you have to think they are good or worship them."

Spur laughed softly. "I've never had a theological argument before with a naked woman."

"Alex used to say never ague with a naked woman, the man will always lose."

"Alex must have been some man. Religions, don't they do some good? What about the moral principals, the standards, the ethics?"

"Those are man manufactured. They have no basis in religion, they are man made. Some of them are commendable. "But don't think that only religion produces ethics and morality. That's a narrow viewpoint of man. Remember the Crusades where hundreds of thousands of innocents were slaughtered all in the name of church? Look at the days of the Inquisition. Those were religious leaders of the Christian Church, notably the Holy Roman Catholic Church, who were tearing those 'heretics' limb from limb for the glory of god. Some god."

Spur smiled. "What about the missionaries, the Catholic priests who went across the Southern U.S. establishing churches?"

"The main purpose of the Catholic Church was to spread the control of the church. Which allowed them to collect more money. To promise the peasants glory in heaven even if they were destitute in this life and gave all their money to the church."

"You are tough on them," Spur said. "No church, no resurrection, no life after death?"

"Of course not! Life after death is a logical contradiction. Does a tree live after you cut it down? Does a horse live after it is shot in a gunfight? Using the same logic neither does a man or woman or child live after they take their last breath. As Alex used to say, they simply cease to exist."

"Like I said, you are tough on religion." He kissed her soft lips and they kissed back. "Since I'm arguing with a naked lady, I can't win. It doesn't matter, I have little use for religion myself. Now what say we get warm by the fire, and figure out what other games we can play?"

They made love three more times that night, then dozed and woke and slept again. Spur kept the fire going to discourage any wandering rattlers, and by morning they were dressed again, but chilled and sore from sleeping on the ground.

"No breakfast," Spur said.

Libby rubbed the sleep out of one eye and sat up. One of her breasts poked out from where she had not buttoned up the front of her dress. Spur bent and kissed it, chewed on the nipple until she pushed him away. "I have a meeting to get to by nine o'clock, can we make it?"

"The Relocation Committee?"

"Yes."

"We'll get there as quickly as we can."

Spur lit two torches, checked his watch and they started to retrace their steps. The time was eight fifteen A.M. They came to the ladder that led up to the next level tunnel and checking closer, Spur saw that the rungs were not in as good a shape as he had thought on the way down.

Two of the cross bars were gone completely, and another weakened. He helped Libby get past the broken one, and soon she was in the tunnel above and off the ladder. He swung up to the next rung but when he put his weight on it, it broke in half and his foot slipped from the rung below. He crashed six feet to the bottom of the shaft and dropped the torch.

"Spur, are you all right?" Libby called. She held the torch down low until she could see him.

"Damn ladder broke," Spur said. I'll try again and spead out my weight more." He left the torch blazing away on the bottom of the shaft and tried the ladder again. This time he stepped on the rungs close to where they were nailed to the uprights, and grabbed them with his hands against the uprights as well.

It worked. He got past the broken ones and crawled over the edge. Libby kissed him.

He took the torch and they worked back the tunnel watching for snakes and shafts. They came to the next shaft and went around it and soon were at the metal stakes between the two mines.

Spur loosened the six-gun in his holster. She looked at him.

"You expect them in this far?"

"This is where I'd be if I was waiting for someone. Catch them before they were ready." They moved cautiously. Spur kept the torch well away from his body and made sure Libby stood on the other side as they walked. A shot at the torch would probably miss his hand and warn them.

They stopped twice to listen, but heard nothing. At last they saw the light from the tunnel opening ahead. Spur put out the torch and they crept ahead cautiously.

At the entrance he edged around at twelve by twelve beam and looked out. Nothing. He saw no movement, heard nothing. No smoke came from the chimney of either building.

He moved back where he had left Libby. "Stay here. I'm going to make a run for the buildings and see if they are waiting for us. There are two of them still alive."

Spur paused at the entrance, then with his six-gun out, he raced out of the tunnel and the twenty yards to the first building.

Nobody fired at him. He looked around. The buggy was still there with its horse still in the traces. Two saddle horses were ground tied near by.

He edged around the building and darted ten yards to the back door of the second structure.

Again nobody fired at him. Inside there was no one except the two dead men. Spur checked the three rooms, then outside and at last holstered his gun and walked back to the mine.

"They've left, Libby. Come on out."

When she left the mine she gave a big sigh of relief and hugged Spur in thanks, then frowned.

"What time is it? We have that nine o'clock meeting in town."

"It's a little after nine now. Sorry it took so long. Better to be a little late than a little dead."

Spur brought around the buggy, checked where he had left the yahoo tied up under the building but

found him gone. He figured the lookout had heard
the shooting, got there too late to help, found the
bound man and they both lit out like their tails were
on fire. He tied the spare horses to the back of the
buggy and headed for town. One more stop at the
end of the lane where he had left his rented horse,
and with her fastened on the buggy as well, they
hurried into town.

It took them a little over an hour to travel the four
miles over the rough mining roads.

Libby thought for a moment about her
appearance. She never went out in public without
her company dress and her hair perfect. Today
would be an exception.

The pale blue dress was mud and dirt splotched.
One sleeve was torn nearly off where one of the
kidnappers had grabbed her. She did not even pause
to wash her face but knew it must be smudged and
dirty. Her hair was a mess. It fell around her
shoulders but in straggles and ropes, and she was
sure it looked as if it hadn't been combed for a week.

But she would testify.

They rode into town and somebody shouted in
recognition and hurried to tell the sheriff that the
most important woman in town had been rescued
from her kidnappers.

Spur drove straight to the town hall where the
meeting was being held. He tied the horse to the
hitching rack and asked someone to take the other
horses to the livery, then hurried inside with Libby.

He was sure they made a grand appearance
marching into the hushed Territorial Senate
Relocation Committee hearing. They looked as if
they had slept in their clothes deep in a coal mine.

Someone was testifying.

"That's Rufus Laidlaw," Libby whispered to

Spur.

Spur helped her sit down in the front row, heard
the surprised whispers of the senators on the panel,
and then walked up to Laidlaw.

"Mr. Chairman, pardon this interruption, but my
name is Spur McCoy, I'm with the United States
Secret Service. I'm here on official business."

"If it could wait, Mr. McCoy, Mr. Laidlaw is
testifying on an important matter."

"You'll have to get a deputation later, sir." He
turned to Rufus. "Is your name Rufus Laidlaw?"

"See here, we're in the middle of an important
matter, Laidlaw said."

"Are you Rufus Laidlaw?" Spur asked again, his
voice a parade grounds bellow.

"Yes," Laidlaw whispered.

"Then by the authority granted to me by the
United States government, I'm arresting you for
conspiracy to commit murder, for kidnapping, for
attempted murder, and for involvement in the
deaths of four men hired by you to commit felonies."

Spur took Laidlaw by the arm, lifted him from the
chair and marched him down the aisle and toward
the door.

Just before they got there, Laidlaw drew a hideout
.38 derringer from under his left arm and fired point
blank at Spur. The round slanted off Spur's big
brass belt buckle and pentrated the side of the room.
Spur staggered back by the force of the blow on his
belt and tumbled to the floor.

Laidlaw surged past him, out the door and down
the street. He still had one shot left in the double
barreled derringer.

Helpful hands lifted Spur. Libby ran up, her face a
mask of fear.

"I'm all right," he shouted. "Which way did

Laidlaw go?'' Several men pointed the way and Spur raced into the street. He saw the fat man lumbering into a store across the street and he rushed that way.

The store was a Chinese laundry. Spur pushed in the door and heard singing from behind a curtain. An elderly Chinese with a skull cap and a long braid looked up expectantly.

"Did a man come through here? Where did he go?"

The old Chinese bobbed his head, bowed and pointed behind the curtain. Spur rushed past the curtain and the singing promptly stopped.

There were a half dozen Chinese women and girls doing laundry in round tubs, others hanging the laundry to dry in the empty building, and other folding sheets and clothing items at a flat table.

"The fat man, which way did he go?" Spur asked.

One of the Chinese ladies smiled.

"No English," she said in a sing song voice.

Spur looked in every possible place, but there was no spot where Laidlaw could hide. Spur ran to the back door and looked down the alley.

Half way down he saw Laidlaw puffing along. He stopped to check a rear door to a business but it was locked. He tried the next and ran inside. Spur was half a block behind him.

The place where Laidlaw vanished was Manny Logan's, a small but classy bordello where some of the best men in town could be found. Spur charged in, saw a staircase for confidential visits. He ran up the steps, knew at once what the place was and began opening doors.

Screams and strings of swear words followed each opening. The fourth room was empty, the fifth had only a girl in a housecoat lounging on a narrow bed.

She smiled at him but he shook his head.

"No tits," he said. She threw a book at him.

Two doors down he found where Laidlaw had been. He had ripped off a window screen and went out the opening to a one story roof below. A couple on the bed humped in the final moments of a mutual climax and they never even noticed Spur.

He slid out the window and down the roof. Laidlaw had dropped off the roof into a wagon and then scrambled to the street and dashed into the general store.

Spur was twenty seconds behind him but as soon as he opened the general store door, a shot exploded inside the store and a slug slammed into the casing beside him.

"One more step and I'll blow this lady's head off!" Laidlaw shrilled. "I mean it. I got nothing to lose and you know it, McCoy. Just one more step and you kill this woman."

"Hold it, Laidlaw. You kill her and you'll hang for sure. Best you get now is ten years. You can do that time while you're planning your next scheme."

"Not prison. My dad used to lock me up in a closet where it was dark and cold. I couldn't live five days in prison where they locked me up."

Spur saw him now, crouched behind the small counter near the money drawer. The woman was standing in front of him, Laidlaw's arm around her throat, the derringer against the side of her head.

"I'll kill her, so help me god! Got nothing to lose. You stand back. Get outside!"

"Can't do that, Laidlaw. I'm a federal law officer. It's my job to take you in. I don't even know that woman. Why should I care if you kill her? Lots of women out here in the west now. Ain't like it used to be twenty years ago."

"You're bluffing, McCoy."

"You shoot her and I shoot you at the same time. You that eager to die? Is there life after death, Laidlaw? I can guarantee that you'll find out if you pull the trigger. You just have one shot left. Ain't like you had a six-gun."

"Damn you, McCoy!"

"You tried to kill me three times, didn't you, Laidlaw?"

"Yes, damn you, one of them should have worked."

"Don't hire boys to do a man's job, Laidlaw. Now put down the gun and live until tomorrow. You interested in the sunrise? You'll never see it you keep that derringer up there much longer. I'm not a patient man."

"Why didn't you just stay out of this town?"

"Lady needed some help. I see why. Give it up Laidlaw."

"I can stand here as long as you can, McCoy."

"But the logic is working on you. You're not stupid. You know how bad your situation is. Why make it worse? And besides, you're not sure about life after death, are you? Want to test it out and see if you're right? Why not give it a try, Laidlaw? You'll either be flying around as a happy ghost laughing at us all down here on earth, or you'll be in a long dreamless sleep from which you'll never wake up. Which is it going to be?"

"Christ! Give me the old time lawman who shot first. All this talk is confusing."

"Just put the little gun on the counter and it all will make sense, Laidlaw. The sheriff just came in the back door. Didn't you hear it close? He'll have his gun on you in about half a minute. He's the kind to shoot first. Make up your mind, now!"

"All right! All right, I'm putting down the derringer. My hands are in the air."

The woman fell against him and slid to the floor in a dead faint.

Sheriff Palmer stepped out of the supply room and eased his six-gun against Laidlaw's neck. His voice surprised the man. His appearance also surprised Spur who had bluffed the idea.

"Easy, Laidlaw," Sheriff Palmer said. "I got a nice cell waiting for you."

Spur walked up and tried to revive the woman.

"McCoy, sometimes I think you're taking all the fun out of being sheriff. We could have had a dandy of a shootout here."

"Right and two maybe three of us would be dead by now."

"Guess you're right," the sheriff said.

"The lady clerk here is damn sure that I'm right," Spur said. "She's one of the ones who would have been dead."

13

Lawrence Taylor watched the disruptive exit of the two men and gaveled sharply on the special board.

"Gentlemen, ladies, we will have order. Close the doors, and come to order. This is a Territorial Committee meeting. The officer was within his rights to arrest the gentleman, now we must continue with our business.

"Mrs. Adams, you were the first witness, and since you were not present when we began, we moved Mr. Laidlaw into your place. If you're ready, we will proceed."

Libby walked to the front of the chamber and sat in the witness chair. For the first time she seemed concerned about her appearance.

"Mr. Taylor, I thank you for allowing me to testify. As you may know I was kidnapped last night by five armed men. They were hired by Rufus Laidlaw specifically to keep me from speaking before this committee. Only now have I returned after spending all night in an abandoned gold mine trying to find my way out.

"I assure you my state of dress and even my dirty face, are no reflection on this committee. I was determined to get here, even looking the way I do.

"What I have to say is important, because it is vital that we move the territorial seat of government closer to the life lines of communication and transportation, and closer to the center of the territory so all sections of Montana can be served. You gentlemen know the geography of our territory. Helena is near the center from north to south, and in the middle of the area which we project will have the greatest population growth.

"One of the largest growth potential elements is the railroad. The Northern Pacific is even now drawing up final plans for its line through Montana, and the best information we have at this stage is that the general route will follow down the Yellowstone River valley to Livingston, then swing west and northwest to Helena.

"I don't need to remind any of you how the presence of a railroad line is a tremendous boon to any community and area, opening it up for trade and for development and as an artery for quick transportation of goods and services to points both east and west. That will make Helena the ideal place for our territorial and we hope soon our Montana state capital.

"I'm sure the mayor and the county board of Commissioners will have a lot to tell you about Lewis and Clark County. Gentlemen of the committee, do you have any questions for me?"

There was one.

"Are you positive about the route of the Northern Pacific through Helena," one of the men on the committee asked.

"I am. I hope the railroad is. If I were a gambling

person, I would put all of my money out right now that the rails will be coming through Helena."

There were no more questions. Libby smiled at the men on the committee. "Thank you, and if you don't mind, I'll go and get cleaned up a little before our dinner at twelve-thirty sharp at my house as planned."

She stepped off the witness stand and walked quickly out of the room.

Irv Nelson, owner, editor-publisher of Helena *Graphic*, called to her as she entered the hallway.

"Mrs. Adams. Do you have time to tell me about what happened on your kidnapping? I want to write a story about it for the paper."

"I really don't have time. The committee is coming for dinner this noon . . ." She paused. "If you'll drive me to my house we can talk. I'll tell you what I know. Then you see Spur McCoy and the sheriff for the rest of it. All right?"

Nelson grinned, helped her down the steps then handed her into the carriage and drove it to her house and into the stables in back just off the alley.

She talked constantly as they drove, and he made notes as fast as he could. At the house he thanked her and she hurried inside to find Charity staring at a box of food that had come from the general store.

"Dinner!" Libby said and hurried Charity and the cook into making a fantastic feast for dinner for the committee as she heated water for a long bath.

If everything worked out right dinner would be on time and she would be clean and combed and dressed before the four men arrived at twelve-thirty.

Spur McCoy had found the sheriff in and pushed all three hundred pounds of Rufus Laidlaw at him. The man was quickly led to a cell and Spur told the sheriff what had happened during the kidnapping, including where he could find the three bodies out at the old Laidlaw mine.

"I'll take your word for the third one. The other two need to be brought in and identified for the record. You say there are still two of the kidnappers free?"

"Somewhere out there. We got Libby back for her talk to the committee. Is it that important?"

"Damned important. I'm going to tell them how the sheriff's department will be enlarged as needed to take care of normal policing activities for the territorial capital, and that we will cooperate in any way with all territorial policing agencies now in place and any that might be created. If we can nail down this relocation, Helena will boom."

"Hope it works out for you." Spur relaxed in a chair in the sheriff's office. "You going to need me for the trials?"

"Damn right. We'll get them set up early, be a week, maybe a week and a half at the most. Without you to testify we have no case."

"Done. Figure I can spend a week or so going after a Grizzly bear. You know a good guide who could get me into Grizz country?"

"Reckon I could scare up one or two. You do any fishing?"

"Some. Guess I'll have enough things to do for a week."

"Make it my business to see that you do," the sheriff said.

Spur stood and stretched. "Guess it's high time I have a bath, and then a nice big dinner, couple of steaks sounds good. Then about a full day of sleep to catch up. You ever tried to sleep in a cold gold mine tunnel with just a little fire and one blanket to keep you warm?"

The sheriff shook his head. "But then you forgot something. You had Libby Adams along as well to keep you warm."

"Yeah, true," Spur said noncommittally and walked out into the sunshine.

He strode with purpose toward the hotel where he figured would be the best spot to take a bath at one of his rooms. As he crossed the street a .44 blasted somewhere ahead of him and a slug slammed over his head and out of town. Spur reached for his gun but saw a man standing thirty yards down the street, the smoking gun still in his hand and aimed at Spur.

"Wet met last night, McCoy. You didn't give me a fair chance. Figure I owe a damn lot to three of my friends so I'm gonna put you out of your misery."

Spur tried to recognize the man, but it had been dark. This would have been the one at the mine that he tied up and pushed under the building.

"You're lucky to be alive. Why don't we leave it that way?" Spur called.

"Not the point. You made me look bad. I was outside. I cost the lives of three of my friends. I won't sleep until I even the score with you."

"You try and there's the chance that you might never sleep again." Spur checked the street, and scanned the buildings on both sides.

"Don't worry, I'm alone. The lookout in the tree you went around lit out for Denver last night. I don't scare nowhere near that easy."

"Do you bleed?"

"You got no choice, smart mouth. I'm putting my iron back in leather. You better get ready. You're packing. Next time I draw, one of us is gonna die. I'm bettin' it's you."

"Mighty big bet. It's your life on the line."

"Done it before, won before. You ready?"

"No way to talk you out of it?"

"Shut up and draw."

The man went for his iron and Spur beat him to the draw, he thumbed the hammer back with his left palm and fired when the six-gun was waist high and still moving upward. The round took the man in the right shoulder and shattered it. The gun spinning out of his hand.

The man roared in pain and hatred. The jolt of the lead bullet had slammed him four feet backward and dumped him on the ground. He crawled to his gun using only his left hand. The man fisted the weapon and turned, but Sheriff Palmer's right boot smashed into his wrist, breaking it and separating the left hand from the gun.

"Don't, son. You'd just be dead, and we need a star witness against Rufus Laidlaw," Palmer said. He looked down the street at Spur. "Didn't tell me you was a gunsharp as well. Thanks for hitting him in the shoulder. He'll talk his head off to stay off a scaffold."

"Just the way we planned it, Sheriff," Spur said and continued on his way toward the hotel, pushing out the spent round and shoving a new one in to complete the five live ones. Never could tell when a body might need five shots.

At the hotel desk he asked for his key and the desk clerk gave him a message in his box. Before he read it he ordered five buckets of hot water and a bath tub brought to his room, then went that direction.

The note was short: "Spur . . . please come to dinner at my house at twelve-thirty. I'm entertaining the Relocation Committee and need your moral support." It was signed, Libby.

Spur shrugged. Why not? The only other problem on his list was the Will Walton ranch, and the killers he was sure were there. They would not be going any place. That changed his plans about a long nap. But he had to eat. Suddenly he realized he was as hungry as a starved caribou.

The bath lasted until the water turned cold. He soaked out the grime and the aches from the night in the mine, then toweled himself dry and dressed in a set of clean clothes he had left in the room so it would look lived in.

He brushed off his low peaked, brown hat, the one with the ring of Mexican silver pesos strung around the crown, and decided after he shaved he would be fit company, even for a Montana Territorial Committee.

He was early. Spur stopped by at the Lewis and Clark county courthouse and talked to the county registrar.

"Yep, found it," the tall, balding man with half glasses said. "Recorded all right here in the book. Owner is listed as Mrs. William (Martha) Walton. Grant deed is free of any incumbrances, no co-owners."

"When was it recorded?"

"Let's see. Date is May twelve of eighteen and sixty-seven. Little over three years ago, seems."

Spur thanked him and strolled to the mansion on the corner with five minutes to spare. The other guests were already there. Charity welcomed him, stepping close to him and rubbing his crotch, then grinning and led him into the parlor where the other four men waited for Libby.

Spur introduced himself again to the men, who welcomed him.

"You get that Laidlaw feller?" one of the men

asked.

"Yes, undamaged and ready to stand trial as soon as the judge can get here."

"Good. He's been a thorn down at the capital. Friend of some sort of the governor, 'though I don't know why."

Libby came into the room and the men all stood automatically.

"Beautiful!" the chairman of the group said. "Now that is what I call a transformation!"

"Is this the same bedraggled woman who testified before us this morning?" another man said.

"Thank you, gentlemen. I warned you this morning I was not in my best state of repair. I'm glad you like the new model."

She had turned with one hip toward them emphasizing her narrow waist and the dress did the rest, plunging between her breasts showing just a hint of each on the sides. Spur was sure she wore nothing under the top of the dress. When she walked forward her breasts bounced and jiggled enticingly and he knew that she had this committee eating out of her carefully manicured hand.

"Dinner is served," Charity said from the door.

"Good, right on time. Gentlemen, this way, and I hope that you're feeling hungry. My poor cook has been up all night getting things ready."

Not true, Spur thought as he brought up the end of the line. She seated him at the far end of the table with the committee chairman on her right.

For a mid-day snack it was something of a banquet.

It began with asparagus soup, moved on to a green salad and then two exquisitely roasted pheasants, each with the showy tail plumes extending from the cooked birds. They had been basted with wine sauce of some sort. Spur was impressed.

Libby charged into her mission. "Gentlemen, is there anything else I can tell you about Helena, the ideal spot for the new territorial capital!"

"Mrs. Adams, I don't think so," the chairman said. "From what you've said, and the prospects prepared by your city council, we were strongly leaning your way anyhow. Then this morning a railroad man said he would give us a hundred to one odds if we wanted to bet that the Northern Pacific rails did not come through Helena."

"That's good enough for me," another member said. "I think the territorial legislature will go along with our recommendation when we get back."

Libby lifted her wine glass. "I propose a toast to Helena, the future capital of the territory of Montana!

They all stood and cheered then drank.

"Now, I have something really serious to talk about. Most of you know that Senator Marlowe introduced my bill in the legislature to give women the right to vote. They have it in Wyoming, used to have it in New Jersey. How come women are second class citizens here in Montana?"

"Mrs. Adams," the smallest of the men on the committee said. "I've read your bill, frankly I'm against it. Most women I've talked to just aren't interested in politics or in the lawmaking process. Women are interested in their homes, their husbands, having babies, and raising them. That's their job."

"Most men are not interested in politics either," Libby countered. "I suppose you know that less than twenty percent of those men eligible to vote do so. That means less than one out of five men are interested. Why not give one out of five women the same chance to send our lawmakers to the legislature?"

"Wouldn't work."

"It does in Wyoming. I went down there during their last election. It worked extremely well. They even have four women elected to the legislature. Are you really saying women are too stupid to be lawmakers?"

"Now, Libby. . . ."

"Am I too stupid? I am currently operating twenty-three business firms here in Helena. True, I inherited them from my late husband. But in the past six years, the net worth of these companies has increased by twenty-seven percent. I have bought six new firms, and have plans for three more. I have more than four hundred employees in this area, most of them men. Am I too stupid to be a legislator?"

"Of course not, Libby," the chairman said. "Granted you have a point, but you also have a majority of the men who don't want women to vote. That's just the way it is. Might take fifty years to change it." He grinned. "But, by god, you keep trying!"

The next course arrived, delicate mountain trout fillets that had been baked and covered with a thick cheese sauce. The men forgot politics and ate.

Spur went around the table and whispered to Libby.

"I have to go. One more little job for me to take care of while I'm here."

"Right in the middle of dinner?"

"Sorry. You push your problem. I'll be back." He said goodbye to the other diners and slipped out the front door.

It took him fifteen minutes to get his horse outfitted, find his Henry repeating rifle, and tie on a blanket roll and a minimum supply of dried rations for an emergency. Never could tell when a afternoon's ride would turn into something longer.

He stopped by the undertaker and left ten dollars for a casket and funeral for Will Walton, then rode for the ranch. It was only a little after one o'clock.

Less than half a mile out of town, Spur checked his back trail and saw a rider there. Lots of people moving around. He went another half mile toward the Walton ranch and kept checking. The rider had turned off the trail when he had and followed him into a heavy wooded section on a small ridge. There was no reason anyone should be going exactly this way unless the man was trailing him.

Spur tied his horse to a tree and backtracked a quarter of a mile at a trot, put the Henry against a ponderosa pine and settled down to wait. Ten minutes later the rider came up fast, monitoring the easy trail Spur had left in the leafmold under the trees.

Spur sent a rifle round over the rider's head.

"Hold it right there!" Spur bellowed.

The rider pulled up.

"McCoy? Is that you? Tried to find you in town, but by the time I caught up with you, you had moved out this way. My name is Kennedy, U.S. Marshal here in Western Montana."

Spur relaxed a minute, kept his rifle ready and stood.

"You afraid of something, or can I lite and talk a spell?" the marshal asked. He had a silver pinned to his leather vest.

Spur nodded. "Lite, but go easy. Far as I know there aren't any U.S. Marshals assigned to Montana

Territory right now. Budget problems they tell us. What was your name again?''

"Kennedy, Marshal Bob Kennedy. I work out of Denver usually. Sent me up here to check on some rustled cattle. But mostly I'm finding gold mines and some Indian trouble.''

"Sounds about right.''

The man had eased to the ground. He had a hogsleg on his left hip and Spur watched him.

"Who's the chief marshall in Denver?'' Spur asked.

"What is this a test of some sort? His name is Chief Marshal Bill Barber, less he's been replaced in the last two weeks.''

Spur grunted. Let the rifle muzzle drop. Barber was the man, but half the west knew about Bill.

"What did you need to talk to me for?'' Spur asked.

"The Laidlaw thing. Just heard. Sounds like you got him wrapped up and tied with a noose.''

"Not quite, but I'll be around to make sure.''

"That's fine. I can get on with my work. Thought I'd offer my services if I could help.''

Spur stood ready, still not convinced. "Thanks, but it's all done. Say, I hear all you marshals got issued new service revolvers, that brand new one from Remington. Like to take a look at it if you don't mind.''

"New . . . Hell not me. I'm the last one to hear about everything. They keep me on the run.''

"Strange. I talked to Bill in Denver three weeks ago, and he said no man would go on assignment without the new weapon. Jody said he had plenty to go around.''

The man shook his head and turned. "Damned if I know what went wrong.'' Then his eyes widened and

his head made a tiny involuntary movement as his
right hand darted to his gunbelt and scratched at
iron.

He was fast. Spur came up at the same time with
his weapon and dove for the protection of the
ponderosa. Both guns exploded black powder,
driving .44 slugs out six-inch barrels. Spur took a
glancing hit on the heel of his boot as he gained the
safety of the three foot tree.

The other man screeched with a round in his left
shoulder. He dodged behind at tree. Spur put a rifle
round close past the tree hiding the imposter.

"No way out, whoever you are. You try to run, I
nail you."

"I won't run. I owe you. Four of my friends you
slaughtered."

"Two matter of fact. One jumped into a pit of
rattlesnakes in the mine. Another one is in jail in
town talking his head off. He said you took off for
Idaho."

"That was the plan. Only I was supposed to
bushwhack you just out of town. You moved too
fast and there warn't no cover."

"The man in the tree out at the mine, that's you."

"Yeah. Made me look bad."

"Try it."

Spur darted to another tree ten feet away and
crouched behind it. The kidnapper heard Spur but
couldn't know where. He edged around the tree and
Spur saw his legs. Spur's rifle round bored through
the outlaw's left thigh and he screamed.

A minute later the man came around the tree
limping, both hands holding six-guns as he stormed
at Spur's tree. He fired as he came, keeping Spur
behind the safe tree. After six shots Spur leaned out
at ground level and fired one round that caught the

kidnapper in the throat and ripped the side of his head off, dumping him to the ground where he twitched a few times, then lay still.

Spur sat up, moved to the dead man and rolled him over. He had done his last kidnapping. Kid looked no more than twenty-five or six. That was seeming younger to Spur all the time. He took the two pistols the man carried, and a rifle from his saddle boot and put them with his gear. He untied the horse and whacked it on the rump. It would wander back to the road and someone would find it. Then he turned and continued on his way toward the Walton ranch.

One more little task to take care of . . . a murderer.

14

Spur lay in a scrabble of brush a quarter of a mile from the Martha Walton ranch. It was truly hers now with the real Will Walton dead. He had been watching for fifteen minutes and the only movement he saw was Hans running quickly from the barn to the side door of the house.

Spur had no real chance to shoot him, and he wanted to talk to the man first anyway. A short time later the boy left the side door and walked to the privy. When he came back he looked all around as if trying to see if someone were riding up. The screen door banged as he went back inside.

Smoke came from the kitchen chimney.

Spur searched for cover closer to the house. The outhouse was too close, the well house too far away in the small gully. Thirty yards on this side of the house lay three boulders big enough to cover a man. Spur mounted up and rode hard out of the brush to the boulders, making turns and changes in speed to throw off any rifle aim.

He had just bailed off his horse when the rifle

spoke. A round went high and by the time the sound had echoed away into the hills, Spur was belly down in the dirt behind the big rocks. Now he was plenty close enough to call.

"Martha Walton inside the house. This is Spur McCoy, U.S. lawman. Your husband is dead, the real Will Walton died in the doctor's office in town."

A shotgun blasted from a crack in the front door but few of the pellets got the thirty yards to the rocks.

"I'm here to take in Hans for questioning. You send him out and we won't have any trouble."

The rifle barked again three times in quick order, which told Spur the man had some kind of a repeater. He ducked lower.

"Before Walton died he told the sheriff that both Hans and Martha were in on the killing."

"No!" a thin boy's voice shouted.

"Ain't so! My mom wouldn't kill nobody!" A defiant Will Walton Junior stood in the open doorway for a moment before a big arm came out and swept him aside and slammed the door.

"Might as well come get us, McCoy," Hans called. "We're not coming out." Another rifle round spanged off the rocks.

"A matter of time, Hans. I got all day. You have a ranch to run. Cow going to need to be milked about five."

The side door swung open and the seven year old rushed out. He ran twenty yards away from the house and hid behind the privy.

"My Ma didn't try to kill my Pa!" the boy shouted. "I know she didn't. She was in the house."

The shotgun roared and the outhouse took the full load of buckshot. The boy was unhurt. Twice the rifle drove rounds into the wooden structure.

"Lay down behind the privy, Will!" Spur called. He sent two shots from his pistol through the window of the house and then motioned to Will, waving him to run for the barn. As soon as Will took off for the barn, Spur pumped his last three pistol rounds at the rear door, then two rifle shots. Two pistol shots came from the house but Will reached the barn safely.

"Send the woman out, Hans. I don't want to hurt her. You're the only one on my arrest order."

Two more rifle rounds answered him.

In the quietness that followed, Spur could hear the couple in the house shouting at each other. The door came open once and was slammed shut.

Again the door swung open and Martha rushed out, looked at the barn, then ran toward the outhouse.

Spur had reloaded his pistol and he sent three shots through the side door. He thought she would make it. Then the rifle in the house spoke sharply and Martha stumbled and fell six feet from the small structure.

Spur used the rifle now, sent the rest of his magazine of rounds through the open door and the window on that side. Quickly he reloaded his pistol and pushed the loaded magazine he had taped to the stock of the rifle, into the Henry with twelve more rounds.

"Give it up, Hans. You'll never get away. Come out and take your chances with a jury. Locals didn't know Will, they might let you off easy."

Spur watched the house. Out of the corner of his eye he saw Martha move slightly, then she lifted and tried to crawl the six feet to protection behind the outhouse.

McCoy fired three times through the back door,

then once more. The rifle inside the house fired twice and Spur saw one of the slugs hit Martha. She screamed, then did not move.

Spur watched the house but saw no movement.

Will Jr. showed himself at the barn door for a moment, saw his mother near the privy and screamed in fury as he ran forward. Spur tried to cover him by shooting at the house, but this time there was no response from inside the ranch house.

Will reached the safe haven and pulled the still form of his mother behind the small building.

The house was too quiet. Spur noticed now that he was masked by the bulk of the house. Someone could go out a back window and get to the corral and then go unseen to the back of the barn.

Spur looked up at the edge of the barn and saw movement. He lifted up and raced to the small outdoor convenience. He dropped to the dirt where Will Jr. held his mother's head in his lap. Tears streaked his dirty face.

Blood showed on the front of her dress. One arm was bleeding.

"Is Ma dead?" Will asked.

"No, she's bleeding." He touched her throat and felt a weak and rapid pulse.

"Mrs. Walton." Spur said. He bent and pinched her face a moment in his hands. "Mrs. Walton!"

Her eyelids fluttered open, closed then opened again.

"It's all right. You're safe now. Will is here."

He bent and kissed his mother. She smiled.

"Will, this is your ranch. You pay heed to what McCoy here says. He's like your Pa. Understand?"

Will nodded through his tears.

"Ma, you got to get well!"

"No, Will. Hurt bad. You take the ranch, and run

it. Make . . . make me proud." She looked at him.
"Inheritance, in the bank in town. Yours, now. Ten
thousand dollars. More coming. From your real Pa's
family. You be a good boy."

He bent and kissed her and when he lifted away
the last earthly breath of Mrs. Martha Walton
whispered into eternity.

"Will, you stay here with your Ma. I'll be back."
He raced for the barn, expected to find Hans gone,
and he was. He looked out the back door and saw a
rider galloping hard for the hills.

Spur ran back to where his mount had been
grazing after he jumped off her, and stepped into the
saddle. He pushed the Henry in the boot and waved
at Will, then rode at a canter toward where he had
last seen Hans.

Hans had proved before that he was no expert
man in the woods, yet he angled toward the first
timber he found. Spur watched the tracks of the
horse and slowed his own. Most horses used west of
the Mississippi could run a quarter of a mile at a flat
out gallop and faster than any racehorse. But then
they had to slow and rest. Spur grimly studied the
tracks, then pushed on.

They went over the bridge, down the other side,
through a small valley and into the timber again.
This ridge had only Douglas fir on it, with hundreds
of small trees sprouting, and making the passage
that much harder. The trail was easy to follow. Spur
knew the man had a rifle, a Sharps maybe, but more
likely a Henry from the sound of it back at the ranch
house.

Spur estimated he had traveled a little over a mile
from the house when he stopped and listened.

The sound came from ahead, a high piercing
scream. The sound of a horse in pain.

Spur picked up the pace, watching carefully now. When he topped the rise he saw the horse below, it had foundered and gone down. The man had simply ridden it to death. It still pawed the ground on the grassy slope. Hans sat six feet away, one of his legs bent at an unnatural angle.

The horse screamed again. Spur dismounted, took out the Henry and steadied the barrel against a fir tree and refined his sight. The rifle spoke sharply in the cool, clear mountain air. The .44 rim fire slug smashed through the air and hit the horse in the head, putting it out of its misery.

Hans screamed when the sound of the shot died.

"McCoy, you bastard! Come and get me. You'll pay if you want to take me in. Ain't one to be in prison. Yanks let me out of a Tennessee prison during the war. Ain't going back to another one."

"Won't be all that hard, Hans," Spur called. Two rifle slugs sang through the air near him. Spur slid behind the fir and peered around. Hans had crawled to cover.

It took Spur fifteen minutes to work his way around the killer near the dead horse. There wasn't much protection there, but he had found a depression and two trees to hide behind. Now Spur had passed the trees and he had the high ground.

The Secret Service Agent put a rifle round into the dirt beside Hans' good leg. The German turned and fired four rounds from his pistol, then began frantically to reload.

"Give up, Hans. Being dead is no fun. Think about it."

Three more rounds powered into the brush over Spur's head, then Hans lay waiting.

Spur made a series of safe moves from tree to tree working the thirty yards down the slope toward

Hans. Spur could have killed Hans a dozen times, but he wanted Hans to hang for Will's death and for Martha's murder.

Spur stepped out from behind a covering Douglas fir ten feet from Hans, his pistol muzzle centered on Hans' chest.

"Drop the iron," Spur demanded.

"No," Hans said. He lifted the gun, swung it past Spur and put the barrel in his mouth.

"I think you're out of rounds," Spur said. "Anyway, that's a coward's way out."

Hans pulled the muzzle out of his mouth and snorted. "Why do you suppose I was in a Rebel prison, I was afraid to fight!" He put the gun barrel back in his mouth, shrugged and pulled the trigger.

Hans died at once. The round tore off the top of his skull spewing blood and bone across the virgin forest. Spur's eyes squinted for a moment, then he moved forward and pulled the pistol from the dead fingers and checked it.

Hans had saved the last round for himself.

A half hour later Spur had taken Hans' wallet for identification and both his weapons, and climbed up the hill to his horse. That was when he checked the Henry repeating rifle Hans had used. It was out of rounds as well.

As an afterthought, Spur rode back to the dead horse and pulled the saddle and bridle off. They belonged to the WW ranch, might as well take them back.

Will Jr. was hard at work digging a grave when Spur rode into the ranch yard. He put the tack in the barn, tied up his horse and took up a second shovel that was beside the just begun grave. It was on a little rise near a cherry tree that had been half frozen off during some hard winter.

Spur hadn't said a word. Will Jr. sniffled now and then, once wiped his nose on his shirt sleeve. Neither of them looked at the body sprawled behind the outhouse.

When they had the grave down three feet, Spur caught Will's shovel.

"Will, be best for you to go in and get some clothes and things together so you can live in town for a while. We'll need to get things sorted out, find somebody to run the ranch, and you'll need to go to school in the fall."

"No more school," Will said quickly. "I got a ranch to run."

Spur dug a few spades full of the rich black soil.

"You want to run the ranch right, do a good job?"

"Sure."

"A smart man will do it much better than one with no book learning. I have a lady in town I want you to meet. She never could have a family. She might like you, keep you at her house and help you with your homework. Way things are these days with the tough competition, a man's got to be as smart as he can to run a big ranch like this."

Will Jr. stared at him.

"What would your Ma want you to do?"

"She always said I had to get a high school diploma. Held real strong to that."

"So there you are, Will."

The lad watched Spur a moment, his big blue eyes steady and the scruff of light hair moving in the breeze. He looked over where his mother lay, closed his eyes a minute and nodded, then turned and walked to the house.

When Spur had the grave dug down five feet he climbed out and found Will dressed in his Sunday best holding his mother's head in his lap. Tears glistened on his cheeks.

"Why did she have to die, Mr. McCoy?"

"I don't know, Will. Things just happen and not always the way we want them to. That's why we have to learn as much as we can so we'll be ready to make the good things happen to us. The more we know, the better we can be sure that we make those good things come."

"Ma never had but the third grade. She said I had to go to school. Only been a little bit so far, we moved around a lot."

Together they placed Martha Walton's body in the grave. Spur said a few words targeted at the boy, not at anything else. Then together they filled in the gaping hole until it was humped up.

Will sat on the porch with hammer and nails pounding together a cross of two by fours.

"I want it to last a long time until I can get a proper marble marker," he said.

They found an ink pen and Spur wrote her name on the cross in strong block letters.

Will insisted on driving the pointed stake of the cross into the mound. Then he dropped the hammer and cried again.

Two hours later, Spur McCoy and Will Jr. rode up to the fence outside of the mansion and tied their horses. Spur untied the suitcase from Will's saddle horn and carried it as they walked up the steps to the big door.

Charity opened it before he knocked.

"We wondered when you were coming back," she said. "Mrs. Adams has been having a stroke." She looked down. "Well, and who is this handsome stranger?"

Spur introduced them and then Libby ran into the entranceway hall.

"Spur McCoy! I've been waiting all . . ." She stopped quickly, her frown turning into a smile as she stared at Will Jr. "I'm sorry, I didn't mean to shout. I didn't know we had real company. And who might this be?"

Will stood stiff and erect. He held out hand as Libby walked up. "How do you do, Mrs. Adams. My name is Will Walton, Jr. and I own the WW ranch outside of town."

Libby dropped to her knees and shook his hand. If Spur thought he had seen her beautiful smile before, he was wrong. Now she had the most marvelous smile he had ever seen and she showered it all on Will. He could see her holding back. She wanted to grab the boy and hug him to pieces.

"Well, young man, how do you do? I'm pleased to meet you. You have your suitcase, I hope you can stay for a while." She stopped. "Say, Charity has been making ice cream in the kitchen, would you like to go with her and see if it's ready to eat yet? She said it should be soon."

"Ice cream?" he said. Then brightened. "Oh, yes! Ma calls it cream. We had some once in Kansas City I think it was. I like it!"

Charity held out her hand. "Let's sample it. We'll be first. We might need to turn the crank a few more times."

Will took her hand and several steps then he hung back and looked at Spur. "Mr. McCoy, is it all right?"

"Sure, Will. Anything Mrs. Adams says is just fine."

Will grinned and they hurried out.

"Will Walton, Jr.?" Libby asked when he was gone.

Quickly Spur told her the story of the disturbed

soldier and how he tracked his missing family here.

"So, Will is all alone. I figured he might be able to stay here for a few weeks until a judge can get it all sorted out and legal. There's also an inheritance of ten thousand dollars in your bank under his mother's name."

"McCoy, you figured get the kid in the house and let her take care of him for a few weeks, and she'd adopt him and never let him go."

Spur shrugged. She caught his arm. "Yes, Libby, something like that. Will has had the raw end of life so far. I figured he deserved a break." He smiled. "And so do you. A kid like that could do wonders for that tough business woman shell you're starting to build up around yourself."

"Why you . . ." She stopped and laughed softly. "I think you're right. First we'll have to find a family who needs work who can run a ranch. Then the ranch will need some more grazing land, probably some good breeding stock from Billings, or maybe from Kansas. Will can live on the ranch during the summers and come in here in the fall to go to school.

"I've been thinking of looking over the school to be sure it has the best possible teachers and materials. There was some talk about needing a new school house as well. I could make a sizeable donation to get it started."

Spur grinned. "Sounds like you're still undecided about Will." He laughed gently. "I've got to go see the sheriff. You save me some of that cream or I'll make another batch myself." Spur hurried toward the front door.

Libby stopped him. "McCoy, you're a schemer."

Spur shook his head. "Not a chance. I'm a dreamer. I figured Will Jr. has had enough hard knocks. Today he watched his mother die and then helped bury her. Not many people have to go through a double emotion blast like that. He's made of good stuff. I know, I saw his father, a hero of the Civil War."

Spur went out the door, set his low crowned hat on his head firmly and hurried to report the deaths to the sheriff.

In the kitchen Will stared around in surprise.

"This whole room is just the kitchen?" he said. "It's as big as our whole ranch house!"

"Yes, Will," Charity said. "And this is the ice cream freezer. Turn the handle and see if it's hard enough." Will tried. He looked up in surprise.

"I can hardly turn it!"

"Good, let's take the top off and taste it," Charity said.

Will watched in wonder as she unlatched the top of the hand crank freezer, took the ratchet off and then lifted the slender metal can out of the ice cold salty water. Carefully she turned the lid and pulled it off.

Soft, pink ice cream showed on the lid and in the can.

"Looks about right," Charity said. She scooped some off the lid with her finger and tasted it. When she nodded and held the lid out to Will he did the same.

"Wow! that is good!"

Libby Adams stood at the kitchen door watching. Things were going to change around her house now. Big changes. Somehow she felt they would be the best days of her life. Here was a brand new human being she could help train and mold and bring up to become a fine man. Somehow she would find a way to lessen his pain and make him remember only the good parts about his mother.

She would treasure these years of watching Will Jr. grow up, and she could pour into him all the love and care she could never give a child of her own. It was like a gift from heaven, even a heaven that she didn't believe in. Libby blinked back the start of a tear and went to sample the ice cream before it was all gone.

15

Spur stepped into Sheriff Palmer's office and spun his hat on his finger. The lawman looked up.

"What this time? You through disrupting this county?"

"Through, Sheriff. You can close the books on the Will Walton shooting. I went out to talk to Mrs. Walton. She and the boy ran out of the house and her hired man, Hans, gunned her down. Little boy saw the whole damned thing.

"By the time I caught up with Hans he had galloped his horse to death in his panic to get away. Hans broke a leg when he went down and couldn't run. Soon as I moved in on him he saved his last round and put it through his mouth."

"God! Least it saves the county the cost of a trial."

"I'll go out with a deputy to bring in the body if you want me to. I put the horse out of its misery."

"Better go out there. Have enough light?"

"We can make it. Oh, I brought the seven year old boy Will Walton Jr. into town. He's staying at

187

Libby Adams' place. Think she might want to keep him there if it's all right with the county."

"Hell, county don't have much say in such matters around here. If it's fine with you and with her and the boy, we'll say good work."

"Done."

Spur and the deputy brought back Hans' body just after dark and turned it over to the undertaker. Whoever his people were would simply never find out what happened to him. He had no papers, nothing to indicate any relatives or a home address. Spur shrugged. It was his choice. He'd never thought much about it, but he decided that a man had a right to end his life if he wanted to. He had no idea why anyone would want to.

Spur rode to Libby's stable and put his horse in a stall, then went in the back door. Libby was still in the living room having a second cup of coffee.

Will Jr. worked on his third dish of ice cream. He had been washed and combed and still wore his best shirt and pants.

"Will and I have been making plans!" Libby said, the eagerness and joy gushing out of her words. "Tomorrow we'll go down town and get some new clothes, and then try and find a bicycle that he can ride. We'll need a pony for him too, and just so many interesting things."

Will kept eating the ice cream. He looked up at Will and grinned once, then finished the dessert.

"I'm going to have to stay around town for a week or two for the Laidlaw trial," Spur said. "Is my welcome still good here, or should I go back to the hotel?"

"You can't run out on me now," Libby said. "Will wants you to go along when we get his clothes."

Spur nodded. "Might work in a fishing trip to one

of the lakes, if you like fishing, Will."

"Yes sir, I'd like that." He looked at Libby, then at Spur. "May I be excused now, please?"

"Of course, Will. You have the rest of the house to explore. We need to pick out which room you want for your very own. Then we'll decorate it and fix it up any way you want to."

"Yes, ma'am." Will got off the chair, looked at both of them and then hurried out of the big dining room.

Spur moved closer to Libby and sat down.

"Don't go overboard on the boy," Spur said. "He's bound to be a little moody for a while. Just lost both his parents, two fathers in two days. Hard to take."

"I'll try to be . . . conservative. But I just want to buy him everything in sight that he wants!"

"He's had almost nothing before this. Go slow and easy. Make do for a few weeks. Do things for him gradually. I talked to the sheriff. He says you can keep Will here if you want to. The county doesn't have any facilities or any money."

"Good!" Libby said.

"Remember, just go slow. Will is coming from a small ranch where they struggled just to get food on the table and to stay warm in the winter."

"Yes, oh wise one," Libby said. "Are you coming to the rally tonight at the church?"

"Votes for women rally?" Spur asked.

"Of course. Eight o'clock. I've invited all the women in the town. But you can come as our security force." She saw his great lack of enthusiasm. "Please, McCoy. I . . . I want you there."

"There shouldn't be any more problems for you."

"I know, that's not why I want you there. I just

want to be close to you when I can. If I let you go
you'd just end up in some saloon pinching the dance
hall girls and playing poker half the night."

"I'll go, I'll go." She went to him and kissed him
quickly.

"We have to leave in fifteen minutes. Do you want
to change?"

"For polite society, I guess I should. I'll come in
after it gets started."

Spur went to the kitchen where Charity had a tray
ready for him with three sandwiches, a pot of coffee
and a big bowl of ice cream.

"Have to eat up the cream before it all melts,"
Charity said. She smiled at him. "You ever get lonesome, give me a call."

Spur ate in the kitchen, heard Libby leave and
then went up to his room and washed up and
changed into a dark suit, string tie and spanking
new low crowned white cowboy hat, and walked
down to the church.

When he stepped inside, Libby was going full
steam ahead.

". . . so the only thing we can do is to flood the
legislators with letters. I write ten letters every day
to various legislators urging them to vote for our
women's rights bill. That's what each of you should
be doing. I've had twenty copies made of the names
and addresses of eight important legislators you
should write to.

"If more of you want the names, please share the
lists. I know we can get the bill passed this session
of the legislature if we push hard on it. I'm going to
Billings and then to Bozeman and Butte and Great
Falls to get women to write letters.

"It doesn't matter if you're no good at writing a
letter. Just tell these men what you want them to

do. Remind them that the hand that rocks the cradle also rocks this territory."

The fifty women in the church applauded politely. A few asked questions and when it was over, Libby thanked everyone and the meeting broke up.

On the way back to her house, Libby held Spur's arm and sighed. "I don't know if we'll ever win. It seems such a hard fight when the men have all the power, the voting power."

"A lot of times money is power, Libby. Did you ever think about that? You could support the men you wanted elected, run a man sympathetic to your cause against men in any district where the man was against you."

"Possible, but our next election is a year away."

"Take you that long to hire a good political consultant, pay him to study the men in the legislature and target the districts you need votes from. And of course get a hundred percent backing by all the districts around Helena."

"Who could I get to do the job?"

"Write some letters to St. Louis and Chicago."

"I'll think about it."

Back at the house, Charity met them at the door. She undid two locks and let them in.

"Will Junior stayed in your library for a while, then he went up to his room, Mrs. Adams," Charity said. "I think he was lonesome and bored."

"I'll go up and talk to him," Spur said. He climbed the open staircase and went down the hall to the smallest bedroom. That was the one Will had picked.

Spur knocked, then went in. Will lay still fully dressed on top of the bed.

"Hi, pardner," Spur said.

"Hello." Will sat up. "There's *nothing to do*

here," Will said. "At the ranch I could feed the chickens, or go for a ride, or just play with my rabbits."

"Give it time. This is your first few hours. Bound to be a little strange. Takes some time to get used to things. You're getting plenty to eat, and that bed looks lots softer than the one I usually sleep on out on the trail. Looks like you found yourself a mighty good place to live."

"But it ain't home, Mr. McCoy."

"That's for sure, Will. But then, I haven't been home to St. Louis even for a couple of years. Two things you need to remember here, seems to me. Book learning. Your Ma was strong about that, you said. And you got to give yourself some time to grow up so you can run the ranch."

"Did anybody milk old Bessie tonight?" Will asked.

"Not sure. I'll ask. Mrs. Adams was going to send someone out to take over running the WW. I'm sure Bessie got drained out right on schedule. Mrs. Adams is an efficient lady. She does things when they are supposed to be done."

Will nodded.

"Just worried about Bessie. I'll need to feed my rabbits tomorrow. Do we have to buy clothes?"

"No clothes tomorrow. You and I will ride back out and check on the ranch."

"Good. I'd like that."

"Now, time for you to get out of your clothes and into that night shirt and dive into bed. Bet you'll sleep good tonight."

"Hope so."

"Will," Spur said. "I'm sorry your real Pa died before you got to know him. He got wounded in the war, shot in the head, and he kept forgetting who he was and even where he lived. He tried to come home, for all those five years he was trying. His head just made it impossible.

"Sorry about your Ma, too. But things are going to be better tomorrow and all the tomorrows after that."

"Hope so," Will said.

Spur waved at him and went out the door. Will was going to make it. Spur had the feeling the young man would do just fine.

Downstairs, Spur found Charity had gone to bed, and Libby sitting in the living room waiting for him.

"How is Will?"

"Scared, still in shock about his Ma being killed that way. Worried about what he's doing here. And homesick. Outside of that I think he'll make it. He and I are going clothes shopping tomorrow, we're riding out to check on the milk cow and to bring back his pet rabbit. We'll make room for the hutch out by the stable."

"Should I look in on him?"

"Not tonight. Let him settle down a little."

"All right. Tomorrow will be much better for him. Glad that is all settled. Now, I'm glad you're staying for a while, McCoy," she said.

"Why?"

"Because you owe me."

"What do I owe you?"

"You owe me a soft, gentle loving in a clean bed with our shoes off and a nip of brandy on the bedstand.

"I try always to pay my debts. Do I bring my own bottle?"

"I can find one and a small snack. In fact, they're already in my bedroom." She kissed him softly on the lips. He kissed her back, only their lips touching.

Her hands fluttered around his shoulders, landed slightly and she leaned against him.

"You'll never know how good that feels, to have a man I like with his hands on me. Could you carry me up to my bedroom?"

Spur scooped her up and headed for the stairs. She nuzzled against his neck, bit him gently and looked up.

"I can be an animal, did you know that?"

"A soft, cuddly animal I hope. Keep your claws retracted." He kissed her nose.

"Alex used to . . ." she stopped. "Never talk about one lover when you're with another one. I forgot the rule."

"He sounds like a smart man, all the way around. He knew you were bright enough to handle his fortune, to run his businesses. He was right. If he could see you right now, I'm sure he would be proud of you."

"He was before he died. I had been managing four firms for about a year. We were in competition with two of his other stores. Usually my stores won. I paid higher salaries, got a key man away from him and we showed more profit."

"Sneaky," he said pushing open her bedroom door. Inside it was a woman's room, nearly twenty feet square, with a canopied bed, a square specially made bathtub built into the corner with a curtain that could be pulled around it.

The scent of sashay drifted to him and the delight of fresh cut flowers in three different vases. The room was decorated with a pink theme, from the soft rug on the floor to the spread on the bed and the canopy over it.

He lowered her onto the softness of a silk bedspread and she sank into the goose down mattress.

"Lay on top of me," she said. "I want to be dominated. Alex was ahead of his time when it came to sex. He said nothing was an unnatural act if both parties wanted to do it. Anything was fine, as long as it didn't hurt and was accepted. He was so smart about everything. He said women didn't always have to submit if they didn't want to. He said most women think it's a duty to fuck their husbands. But it shouldn't be that way.

"Alex said the woman should be having as many thrills as the man in sexual intercourse. I agree. I enjoy sex, don't you?"

Spur grinned, bent down and blew hot breath through her dress onto her right breast. She giggled.

"Yes, I enjoy sex. It's the most intimate, satisfying and delightful experience that two people can have together. Does that kind of talk excite you?"

"Yes."

"I want your body. I want to see it all bare and pink and trembling and I want you panting, just eager as hell for me to ravish you."

"Ravish! what a wonderfully exciting word. Are you starting to ravish me yet?"

"It's a slow ravish. First I open your dress, like this.' He undid buttons down the front. "Then my hands *violate* your breasts."

"Call them tits, tits is a good word."

"Then my hands grab your big tits."

"Now it seems like you're starting to violate me." Libby giggled like a stranger. "Damn, I wish I were a virgin again. I wish it had been someone like you."

He spread back her dress top and pushed aside the silk chemise. Her breasts, even when she lay on her back, were full and heavy. The pink areolas tinged a darker shade now, as her heart raced.

"We were both sixteen and on a church picnic and got lost in the woods and we started exploring each other's bodies. He was a virgin too, he told me later. We both were just curious as hell. We just fumbled around and tore off clothes and got more and more excited until I wouldn't let him stop. It hurt for just a minute, then bliss!"

"Take off your dress," Spur commanded, rolling away from her. "Get it off now!"

She blinked, then sat up and pulled the dress off over her head and three petticoats. She had on the silk and lace panties again, all loose and enticing.

Slowly she undressed him, and soon they were both naked and lying side by side on the bed.

"The first time?" he asked.

"Dominate me. On top and hard and fast. Don't wait for me, make me catch up."

He plunged into her a moment later and she gasped at the burning of the dry flesh against dry, then it eased and he slammed into her again and again. She scowled for a minute, then laughed and ground her hips against him in a furious race to catch up and did at last and then sped past him, exploding before he could.

She yelped and squealed and bounced and made him lose his rhythm, then she faded into a series of long, sharp spasms that left her drained.

Just as she finished he went over the top and powered his seed deep into her and then fell exhausted beside her on the soft bed.

"You won," he said when he could talk. They lay there in each other's arms for ten minutes. Softly she cried, but he didn't ask her why. Another three or four minutes and the tears ceased and she brushed away the last of the wetness and rolled over on top of him.

"Sometimes when it's tremendously wonderful, I just have to cry. I wonder if you can understand?"

"No, not being a woman, I could never understand that one. But I can agree that it has validity and meaning for you. Does that come close enough?"

"Close enough." She kissed him. "I'm going to do everything I can to keep Will here, and make him happy. Makes up for some of the joys I've missed."

"There will be some tears as well, goes with the territory. Just no way to have one without the other."

"I realize that and accept it. I'm going to do everything possible to make Will's life here more joy than tears."

"Good, where's the brandy."

She motioned to the bedstand. He rolled out of the bed and brought it back with two glasses. Spur poured two fingers in each glass and handed her one.

"Medicine for the strong hearted."

"My kind of medicine," she said then leaned forward and nuzzled her ear. "You ever think of settling down somewhere? Letting someone else chase the bad guys?

"Thought of it."

"Always a chance you could find some young widow lady with more money than she could rightly know what to do with. Might even get into bed with her." Libby took one of his hands and put it on her breasts.

"You could probably ravish her if you tried, and the lady could work out a joint venture of some sort, like general manager, or chief executive officer. She would have an adopted son to mother and to tutor and to raise."

He bent and kissed both her breasts and she made small noises in her throat.

"That kind of a set up would be damn hard to find. Might not be more than one in the whole wild west."

"Just what I was thinking," she purred. "We seem to think a lot alike. We could always talk about it."

He sucked half of one of her breasts into his mouth and worried it for a minute, then let it go.

"I don't feel much like talking right now. Any other ideas?"

"One but you might not like it."

"What's that?"

"On the floor with my ankles on your shoulders. If you're ready."

"Hell, woman, it's been ten minutes, I'm ready!" They both laughed and left the bed for the soft pink rug.

"You will think about it, about that sexy widow with the money and a real need in her life that needs to be filled."

"Yes, I'll think about it." He spread her legs and drove forward hard. "I wonder if this will help fill her need?"

Libby giggled and then lifted her feet and put her legs on his shoulders as Spur adjusted forward and watched her get ready to shatter herself to pieces.

He stopped moving.

"What are you doing?" she asked.

"You said I should think about it. I'm thinking."

"Damn you, not now! I've got a much more urgent problem for you to solve than that other. This is a problem that has to be penetrated completely to be evaluated."

He stared at her unsmiling.

"McCoy, if you don't keep on fucking me deep I'm going to crown you good!"

Spur laughed and continued. "Just checking to see if you had dropped off to sleep yet."

She hadn't. Neither of them did until almost three in the morning.

16

Spur woke at five-thirty as usual the next morning and completed a fast needed half mile walk around town. When he returned he found Libby in a dressing gown pacing the living room, her hair uncombed, tears showing on her face.

"He's gone! Will Junior left sometime last night. Nobody heard a thing. He's just gone."

Spur took her into the kitchen, poured a cup of coffee for her and added a shot of whiskey and watched as she drank it.

"He's alone and scared and doesn't really know who his friends are yet," Spur said gently. "He's probably gone back to the ranch. Have you checked the horse he rode in on yesterday?"

She shook her head. Charity found his door open that morning when she got up to help the cook with breakfast.

Spur went to the stables behind the big house and found one stall empty. All had been filled last night. Will was too small to saddle a horse. One bridal was missing. He could probably ride bareback as well as with a saddle.

Back in the house, Spur told the women. "Give me a cup of coffee and about six of those cinnamon rolls and I'll go take a look. Chances are, he's back at the ranch by now, depending when he left.

"Explain to him . . ." Libby began, then stopped.

"Yes, Libby. I'll try to explain. Will had a lot of things pushed on him all at once. Remember, we talked about going easy, slow with him? That is more important than ever now. If I find him we'll be back only if he wants to come. We can't make him stay in town if he doesn't want to."

"I sent a family out late yesterday afternoon to run the ranch. He's a former rancher who lost his spread in an Indian raid. He's a good man. Name of Kingman, Frank Kingman. Couple and two kids . . ."

"But you'd rather Will stayed with you than with the Kingmans. I know. I'll see what I can do. Stay busy." Spur took the wrapped rolls and saddled his horse and rode away toward the ranch. He wasn't sure what he was going to say when he got there.

Chances were good that Will would be there. Will might try to set it up to stay with the foreman's family. Such things were fairly common.

Spur rode for half an hour toward the ranch. He had just turned into the long valley from which the finger valley extended where the Walton ranch lay, when he saw the Indians.

There were six, obviously a hunting party on their horses with hackamores and barebacked. Each brave carried a lance and two had rifles. The six sat motionless on the brow of a small hill, outlining themselves plainly.

They wanted him to see them. They were probably Crow in this part of Montana. He rode toward them at a canter to let them know he was not afraid and was eager to talk with them.

The six remained in position and an older brave came from behind them on a large white horse that pranced and skittered as if it was not used to being ridden. The old Indian put the animal under control with soft words and by rubbing its neck. Spur stopped and the Indian stopped. They were ten feet apart.

Spur used the universal Indian sign for welcome or hello and waited. At last the old Indian gave the same sign, his hand raised, fingers straight palm outward.

The Indian looked pointedly at Spur's Henry rifle in his boot, then lifted both his hands to his forehead and made buffalo horns. It was the sign for buffalo.

Spur shook his head no, then held his first two fingers of his right hand outward in a "V" against his left eye. He had not seen any buffalo.

The old Indian sighed, nodded. Then he touched his thumb to his chest indicating himself and with his palm upward, he moved his hand back and forth in front of him.

It was the sign for "go" Spur knew. He nodded and turned his horse and rode away at a slow walk, to prove his bravery by exposing his back to six potential enemy.

The Crow were comparatively at peace with the white settlers. The Indians kept to the higher hills and valleys and left most of the whites alone. Now and then there would be a raid for horses and to capture rifles and ammunition. But it was a time of peace with the Crow in that corner of Montana.

Spur rode a quarter of a mile then looked back. The six hunters had vanished, only the old Crow sat on his horse watching the white man.

Spur thought little more about it as he moved on
down the trail toward the Walton WW ranch. He
had seen fresh tracks in the dust. These were of an
unshod horse and the insects and worms of the night
had made no tracks through the hoof prints. The
prints had been made in late night or early morning.

He came to the ranch as before, saw smoke over
the chimney in the virtually windless morning, and
rode on down.

Will met him before he could dismount.

"Had to come back and check on Bessie," Will
said.

"Figures," Spur said. "How are your rabbits?"

"Hungry. I fed them." Will watched Spur. "You
come to haul me back to town?"

"Nope. Came to see if you were all right. Libby
was worried about you. Just like your Ma would
have been if you ran off."

"She's rich, she doesn't have to worry."

Spur chuckled. "Will, the rich people worry about
more things than we do. They have more reasons to
worry. She likes you, Will."

"She's a nice lady . . . but I'm a rancher. I have
this spread to run."

"She sent out a man and his family to do that for
you, Will."

"I met them. But I can do it myself." Will glanced
up at Spur who said nothing. "Well, I can." He dug
one toe into the dirt. "With a little help, I can. This
man, Mr. Kingman, doesn't know where the stock
is, or anything."

"You going to help him?"

"Soon as I milk Bessie. Come on."

Will led him to the barn and took an upside down
milk pail off a wooden rack. He put a three legged
stool beside a red and beige milk cow and sat down

and cleaned off her udders. Then he began milking her with sure, steady pulls. The milk splashed on the side of the bucket, then into the bottom, churning into a froth of bubbles.

An old yellow Tom cat strolled up and sat down. He meowed once and Will looked at him and grinned.

"You ready, Yaller?"

The cat meowed again. Will turned one teat toward the cat and sent a long stream of warm milk squirting his way. The cat adjusted easily, caught the stream of milk in his mouth and when it stopped coming, he swallowed, licked off the drips on his fur and walked out the other side of the stall making sure everyone knew that he owned the whole spread.

"That old cat's got you trained mighty good, Will. I bet you could bring him back to town with you, if you're thinking of going back. I keep thinking what your Ma said about you getting a diploma and all."

"Yeah, I think about that, too."

He finished the milking, and carried the two gallons of milk back to the house. Inside he introduced Spur to Molly Kingman and their two boys, who were six and seven.

"You had your breakfast, Mr. McCoy?" Molly asked. She was in her late twenties, already starting to show the strain and wear of a ranch wife's hard life. Her smile was open, honest.

Spur said he had eaten, thanked her and said he'd be glad to take a list of supplies she needed when he went back to town and have them sent out on a wagon. She smiled and began deciding what to ask for and writing things down with a stub of a lead pencil.

Will tugged Spur outside to see his rabbits. He had a pair and hoped he would have young ones soon.

"I better clean out the cage," he said. He brought fresh straw and moved the pair of large white rabbits to a second cage.

Will reached into the hutch with a rake to pull out the used straw when he yelped.

"Mr. McCoy, come quick!"

Spur looked where Will indicated and saw eight small, wiggling, nearly hairless newborn rabbits.

"Well now, you're a grandfather!" Spur said. "Best get the mother back in there and keep the buck in another cage. Sometimes the male will kill the youn'ens."

Will's face held a brilliant smile as he tended to the newborns, moved the females back and put out feed. He found some leaf lettuce in the garden and fed them both by hand.

A man left the barn and moved toward them. He was medium height, solidly built and wore a straw hat. He had a friendly face that was weathered. He held out his hand.

"Howdy, you must be Spur McCoy who Will has been talking about. Glad to have you here. I'm Frank Kingman. Will says he's going to show me where the stock is, and where the property boundary lines are. Good thing to know."

"Morning, Frank. Will just got himself a litter of rabbits."

"Fresh rabbit fryers in two months!" Will said.

Frank laughed. "Now there is a real rancher. Knows we produce critters on a ranch to feed bellies."

Will grinned.

"Will, this be a good time to go for our ride around the spread?" Frank asked.

"Sure. Mr. McCoy, can you come, too?"

It took them three hours to ride the ranch, poke into the spots where the cattle congregated, and to roust a few out of some brambles. When they got back, the hundred and sixty acres looked to Spur to be a beautiful little spread. Plenty of water from the stream, lots of good basic sod grass and meadows of wild grass that could be cut for hay.

At the house, the noon meal was ready and Spur sat down with the family.

Molly had a long list of basics she needed. Will finished eating as the adults talked, and went outside with the boys. Spur and Frank smoked black, thin cheroots in the living room, then Spur went out to find Will.

He was kneeling down, sitting on his feet at his mother's grave. Spur came up and sat on the grass beside him.

"Seems a long time since yesterday morning," Will said. Tears splotched his cheeks.

"Long time," Spur said. "I know you loved your mother, but now that part of your life is over. Time to move ahead, to take on new things, to go to school and prepare yourself to run your ranch, the WW."

"I know. I wanted one last look. Mrs. Adams said she would get me a tutor to help me catch up with my grade. I don't want to start in first grade, I'm seven."

Spur nodded. "Figures. Now, we better see about taking the rabbits back to town."

Will shook his head. "Nope. The boys want to take care of them. I gave the rabbits to the boys. They need something of their own here. But . . . could we take Yaller back? He might like it in town."

Spur grinned and they went to find a cardboard

box they could carry the scrappy old tom cat in.

An hour later they had just topped a small rise when twelve Indians formed a line across the trail. All had rifles or bows and arrows in hand.

For a moment Spur sensed danger. Then the line of braves continued down the ridge without a second look at them. One of the Indians was the old hunting chief Spur had talked to that morning. In the valley on the far side of the rise, Spur saw a herd of about twenty buffalo grazing. They were the first he had seen in this area. Evidently the Indians had been tracking them and lost them in the night.

Now they moved slowly down the hill through the pine trees getting in position to attack the herd. The braves were upwind from the buffalo so the beasts could not smell the man scent.

Spur stopped and moved with Will forward where they could see the attack.

"One day soon the buffalo will be gone off the plains and out of the mountains, too," Spur said. "Watch this, you can tell your grandchildren about it."

Nothing happened for a half hour. Yaller yowled and Will talked to him and petted him through a slit in the top of the box.

Below the buffalo wandered closer to the edge of the timber. Then without warning the old bull leading the pack snorted and bellowed a call of danger.

Within two or three seconds, three rifles blasted. Two of the shaggy beasts near the center of the group went down. The others charged away toward the opening of the valley. The Indians streamed after them, six ahead of them trying to cut off their escape, firing at the lead bull who charged directly over one Indian pony without stopping. The brave dove off the horse at the last second and rolled out of the path of the sharp hooves.

The thunder of the hoofs continued for several seconds, as a dozen more shots stabbed through the still mountain air, then all was quiet. The braves who had ridden after the herd came back. Three of the shaggy animals lay still on the grassy valley. At once two of the braves rode off to the north to direct the squaws and ponies with their hunting camp equipment back to the site.

Before darkness, the small band of Crow would have set up a hunting camp, and have butchered out the first animal.

"These Indians get almost everything they need to live on from the buffalo," Spur said. "Robes to keep warm, skins to cover their tipis, food, dried jerky for winter. They use every part of the animal."

The pair rode on, and arrived at Libby's house in Helena just before dark.

Will dashed into the house and found Libby in the living room. It took him a half hour to tell her about the birth of his new bunnies and then how he and Spur had watched the Indians hunting buffalo.

When he was done they had supper and he was still talking.

At last she touched his hand.

"Will, have you decided to stay here in town?" Libby asked.

"Yes. I . . . I guess so. Ma told me to get book learning. This is the only place. If you can put up with me and Yaller."

Libby had been surprised by the cat, but they had put it in the basement along with food and water so he would get used to the area and know where home was.

"Will, I think I'll be able to get along with both of

you. Try not to be too hard on me. Mr. McCoy has to stay in town for a while to go to the trial. I remember he promised you a fishing trip."

"Yes," Will said looking at Spur. "We're going tomorrow. Then the next day we're going to ride into the mountains and try to shoot a grizzly bear!"

Spur laughed. "The fishing sounds fine, but the more I think about the old grizzly, the more I've decided to let him stay up there in the hills. I don't have a fight with any of them."

Spur and Will played dominoes that night. He thought about St. Louis and the office there. He'd have a week here for the trial, which he figured would last about two hours once the judge came to town and it got started. That was the way most trials went out west. No long harangues, no fancy lawyers, just meataxe law that was usually fair but always quick.

Then he'd be back at work. He wondered just where he would go next? First he'd have to get to a telegraph and report in.

His biggest regret on this job had been Will Walton senior. He had been a true victim of the horror of the Civil War. He was killed by the war just as surely as if he had fallen at the Wilderness. May he rest in peace.

Spur remembered Will Junior. He was going to do fine in town with Libby. He'd spend summers at the ranch, and winters in town. If he was as sharp as his Pa, Will would do just fine.

Spur grinned and relaxed. Between Will during the day, and Libby and Charity at night, he was going to have an interesting week!